THE KARMA OF LOVE

THE KARMA OF LOVE

BARBARA CARTLAND

THORNDIKE
CHIVERS

This Large Print edition is published by Thorndike Press, Waterville, Maine USA and by BBC Audiobooks Ltd, Bath, England.

Thorndike Press is an imprint of Thomson Gale, a part of The Thomson Corporation.

Thorndike is a trademark and used herein under license.

The text of this Large Print edition is unabridged.

Other aspects of the book may vary from the original edition.

Set in 16 pt. Plantin.

LIBRARY OF CONGRESS CATALOGING-IN-PUBLICATION DATA

Cartland, Barbara, 1902–2000.
  The karma of love / by Barbara Cartland.
    p. cm. — (Thorndike Press large print candlelight)
  ISBN 0-7862-9077-3 (alk. paper)
    1. Great Britain — History — Victoria, 1837–1901 — Fiction. 2. India — Fiction. I. Title.
PR6005.A765K37 2007
  823'.912—dc22   2006029416

BRITISH LIBRARY CATALOGUING-IN-PUBLICATION DATA AVAILABLE

Published in 2006 in the U.S. by arrangement with Cartland Promotions.
Published in 2007 in the U.K. by arrangement with Cartland Promotions, c/o Rupert Crew Limited.

U.S. Hardcover: ISBN 13: 978-0-7862-9077-2; ISBN 10: 0-7862-9077-3
U.K. Hardcover: 978 1 405 63910 1 (Chivers Large Print)
U.K. Softcover: 978 1 405 63911 8 (Camden Large Print)

Printed in the United States of America on permanent paper
10 9 8 7 6 5 4 3 2 1

AUTHOR'S NOTE

On March 30th, 1885 the Russians attacked the Afghans in a border foray called 'The Battle of Murghab' and occupied the Panjdeh oasis. This brought Britain and Russia to the brink of war.

Some years later a holy man known as 'the Mullah of Swat' or more frequently 'the Mad Mullah' inflamed the whole frontier. Frenzied tribesmen thronged to him in their thousands. After great losses in killed and wounded, villages and crops destroyed, the Mullah fled and his followers surrendered.

CHAPTER ONE

1885

"You can get out and stay out! I'm sick to death of having you in the house looking down your nose at me and setting yourself up as if you were someone of importance. You're a nobody! Do you hear me? Nobody! Let's see how you fare without money and without me to look after you! If you freeze to death, all the better!"

As she was speaking, the Countess of Lyndale, a large, fat, blowsy woman, thrust forward the girl she was holding by the arm so that she fell through the doorway onto the step outside.

The door behind her was slammed.

Lady Orissa Fane remained for a moment lying on the doorstep, conscious that her head was spinning from a blow her Stepmother had given her on her head, and that her arm was painful for the grip of fat, yet strong fingers.

She had been dragged from the Sitting-Room at the back of the house through the Hall and out through the front door.

It was impossible to fight against the Countess when she was drunk, as Orissa had discovered on previous occasions.

But never before had her Step-mother literally thrown her out of the house. Usually she had been able to escape upstairs to her own bed-room, and as the Countess in an inebriated state was unable to climb so many stairs, Orissa had been safe.

The row had started over nothing.

The Countess had always disliked her step-daughter and regularly accused Orissa of "looking down" on her.

Of humble origin and the widow of some petty official in the Indian Civil Service, she had managed with consummate cleverness to capture the Earl when he was returning to England bereaved and desperately lonely after the death of his wife.

The long voyage had given Mrs. Smithson an excellent opportunity to show the widower a warm enveloping sympathy which he had found in some degree comforting.

The Earl of Lyndale had always been a very reserved man and apart from having been extremely happily married, had very little knowledge of women.

Mrs. Smithson, flamboyant, seductive and in those days good-looking, had managed to ingratiate herself to such an extent that three months after they arrived in England she had achieved the supreme triumph in her life when she became the Countess of Lyndale.

Orissa used to wonder whether, if she had been travelling with her father, she would have been able to prevent what proved to be a catastrophe not only for him but for herself.

But as she grew to know her Step-mother and realise that she had an iron-determination and an obstinacy that was unshakeable, she doubted if anyone, least of all herself, could have kept her father from being involved with such a woman.

"If only Papa could have stayed in the Regiment!" she had often said miserably to her brother.

Unfortunately his succession to the title while he was serving in India had made it imperative that the new Earl should return to England to make investigations concerning the state of the family fortunes.

It did not help him to discern on arrival there was practically nothing remaining!

His brother, whom he succeeded to the

Earldom, had run through the small amount of money that had been left them by their father.

Mrs. Smithson found that while she might bear an honourable title, it did not really compensate for the pinched circumstances in which they had to exist, and the lack of servants.

Here however she could make use of her step-daughter and she proceeded to do so.

To Orissa her life became a nightmare from the moment her mother had died in India and she had been snatched away at ten years old from not only the only world she knew and loved, but also from her Ayah who had looked after her from babyhood.

She had been sent home to England ahead of her father because a Colonel's wife who was leaving on an earlier ship had promised to take care of "the poor, motherless child."

To Orissa England seemed a cold, dark and miserable place in which she shivered and ached for the sun-shine which in retrospect seemed part of her mother's love.

At night in her cold little bed-room she would pretend she could hear the comforting noises of India, the chatter of sing-song voices, a baby crying, pariah dogs barking, the creak of the water-well.

"Mama . . . Mama . . ." she would cry into her pillow.

It was her Step-mother who encouraged her father to drink away his troubles, having found in her previous married life it was a panacea for all ills.

Even when she was drunk the Countess seldom spoke of her first marriage, but over the years Orissa gained a very different picture from the one Mrs. Smithson had presented so skilfully to the Earl when they had mingled their tears on board ship and talked sorrowfully of their joint bereavements.

It was excusable in the heat of India to find drink a solace, but in England it could destroy the health and character of those who, like the Earl and his new wife, drank constantly and continually.

It was Orissa who suffered most.

Not only was she in effect an unpaid servant in the tall, ugly house in which they lived in Belgravia, but she also had to endure the shame of seeing her father incapably drunk night after night and her Step-mother behaving like a virago.

No decent servant would stay in the house and the few friends the Earl had in England soon ceased to call.

Orissa found herself cut off from companions of her own age and even from contact with ordinary people.

It would have been a life almost of solitary confinement for the child if her brother, Viscount Dillingham, had not insisted that she should be educated.

He was with his Regiment in India and he had returned home on leave to say in no uncertain terms that Orissa must either go to school or that a governess should be engaged for her.

Fortunately the idea of another woman in the house was more than the Countess could tolerate, and Orissa was therefore sent to a Seminary for Young Ladies not far from their home.

She felt of course that she was an outsider.

Having been brought up in India, she had no idea of what kind of things interested English girls, and the fact that she could never ask her friends to her home made it difficult for her to accept their hospitality.

She did however learn a great deal.

Her reports, which no-one read, often spoke of her as brilliant, especially in the subjects which she liked such as History, Literature and Geography.

On going to school she also discovered that by reading she could escape from the grumbling, bullying and what amounted to both mental and physical cruelty of her Step-mother.

There were no books at home. The Countess glanced through "*The Lady*" and "*The Gentlewoman*", and her father took "*The Morning Post*". Otherwise no literature of any sort ever entered the house.

It took Orissa some time to discover that there was such a thing as a Lending Library, but it is doubtful if she could ever have persuaded her father, who by now was completely dominated by his wife, to pay the subscription.

However her Uncle, Colonel Henry Hobart by chance gave her a year's subscription as a Christmas present. Orissa's effusive and almost overwhelming gratitude had moved him so much that he had renewed the membership year by year.

But even he had no idea that he had thrown his niece a life-line which kept her from sinking into the black depths of hopelessness.

What did not improve Orissa's existence was the fact that, as she grew older, the Countess became jealous of her appearance.

She had always disliked the small fragile child with whom she had nothing in common. But that Orissa should become attractive to the point when people referred to her as 'beautiful' was infuriating to a woman who was well aware that middle-age and too much drink had completely destroyed her own good looks.

Her cruelty to her step-daughter increased with the amount of gin she consumed.

It was then that all the hatred and resentment that seethed within her came to the surface, culminating, Orissa thought now, in this moment when her Step-mother had thrown her outside the front door.

She rose to her feet and shook her skirts free of the soft snow which lay on the steps to the house.

She was conscious as she did so that it was extremely cold, and the fact that she was wearing an evening gown made her position more precarious than it might have been otherwise.

She looked behind her at the closed front door with its badly cleaned brass knocker and wondered what she should do.

To knock on the door would be useless.

The only person who would hear it would be her Step-mother, and in her present state of fury she would have no intention of opening it.

By this time the two inadequate servants would have gone to bed on the top floor and their window faced the other way.

14

Even if they heard her calling, Orissa thought, it was unlikely they would come downstairs, fearful of upsetting the Countess when she was in one of her rages.

'This means I have to find somewhere to go,' Orissa told herself.

She tried to think, aware that her head seemed still to be ringing from the blows which the Countess always aimed at her when she was incensed.

It was at that moment that unexpectedly, because Eaton Place at night was usually very quiet, she saw a hackney-carriage stop two doors further up the road and a man alight from it.

He paid the cabman and walked up the steps to the house. The cabman transferred the money into his pocket, then tightening the reins whipped his tired horse into action.

The cab had actually to pass Orissa and impulsively she put up her hand.

"Cabby!"

The cabman drew his horse to a standstill.

When he looked down from his box-seat at Orissa, there was an expression in his face which she knew was only to be expected.

Ladies did not walk about the streets at eleven o'clock at night unaccompanied and in evening dress.

"Where d'you want to go?" the cabby asked grudgingly, and Orissa knew he was in two minds whether or not to take her as a fare.

"I should be very grateful," she said, "if you would be kind enough to convey me to 24, Queen Anne Street. It is behind Wellington Barracks."

Her quiet, cultured voice seemed to reassure the cabman that she was not the type of woman he had first supposed, and before he could get down from his box, Orissa pulled the cab door open and climbed in.

She sat down on the black leather-covered seat thankful for the moment to be out of the cold and conscious that she was already shivering.

Some of her discomfort was obviously due to her Stepmother's behaviour and the violence with which she had been handled.

She gave a deep sigh and sat back.

Charles would not be pleased to see her but there was really no-one else to whom she could turn at this time of night. So she must go to him and ask his help.

Her brother had arrived home from India but a week earlier and she had only seen him once.

He had in fact been so busy that she had not had time to tell him how desperate things had become in the house at Eaton Place or how intolerable was her existence.

Viscount Dillingham had returned to England, not on leave but because he was to be sent to join the British Expeditionary Force which, having landed in Egypt in September was making unaccountably slow progress up the Nile to relieve General Gordon at Khartoum.

"It is a great opportunity!" Charles had said to his sister, "I am looking forward to it tremendously."

"But it will be dangerous!" Orissa protested.

"All war is dangerous," he answered with a smile, "but it will be a change from India and a real war is something I have longed to take part in."

"Oh, Charles, please take care of yourself," Orissa begged. "If anything should happen to you I would have . . . no-one left."

Charles had hugged her. Orissa had been waiting only until she saw him again before she told him her troubles.

It had been decided that the officers who were to reinforce Lord Wolseley's army which had barely reached the Sudan were to undergo a special intensive course of instruction on the difficulties they had to face.

As Wellington Barracks could not accommodate them all, the War Office had found them accommodation nearby in Queen Anne Street.

"They are bachelor apartments," Orissa thought to herself now. "Perhaps I shall not be allowed in."

For a moment she wondered desperately what in that event she should do. Then she realised that at least she would be able to send Charles a message, and provided he was at his lodgings and not out at a party he would be able to help her.

It seemed to her that the cabman took a long time to reach Queen Anne Street, and when they at last arrived there she remembered thankfully that she had a little money with her.

One of the new maids engaged by her Step-mother was light-fingered. She was young, only a girl of sixteen, and she did not take jewellery or clothing, but any coins whatever their value, left in a drawer or on a dressing-table vanished immediately.

Orissa, who had no money of her own to spend, and was only able to keep herself clothed by extracting a few pounds from her father at irregular intervals when he was in a good mood, could not afford to lose even a few pennies through petty pilfering.

She had therefore taken to carrying her purse about with her even when she went down to dinner. She drew it now from the pocket of her red dress and found with relief that she would have enough to pay the cab.

'It is extraordinary,' she thought to herself as she did so, 'how things turn out for the best!'

She had thought that the maid's habit of stealing was a nuisance when she had to add a pocket to every dress she possessed.

As she made her own clothes it had not been a very difficult thing to do, and now it had proved to be a blessing in disguise, for it would have been even more difficult to arrive at Charles's lodgings and have no money with which to pay the cab.

The horse came to a standstill, Orissa alighted and asked the fare.

She gave the cabman what he required and a tip, for which he touched his hat, then she ran up the steps of the house in front of her.

The door was open and she found in a small hall there was a soldier in uniform seated at what appeared to be a kind of Reception desk.

He looked at her in surprise and she realised that he thought it strange that anyone should come in out of a cold night in January without a wrap of any sort.

"I want to see Viscount Dillingham," Orissa said.

"Second floor, Ma'am. Name's on the door," the soldier answered with a military briskness.

"Thank you," Orissa said and started up the stairs.

They were steep and as Orissa turned onto the first landing a man came out of one of the rooms and she almost bumped into him.

He was tall and was wearing a blue Mess jacket with a red braided waist coat. He not only appeared surprised at her presence, but stared at her in a manner which in other circumstances she would have thought offensive.

In some embarrassment she quickly turned her head away and hurried up the next flight of stairs. But not before she had realised that the man's grey eyes in a thin, sun-burnt face were uncomfortably penetrating.

She had the feeling without looking back that he was standing watching her until she was out of sight.

This forced her to hurry so that she was breathless by the time she reached the second floor and saw a card pinned on one of the doors on the landing — "Captain Viscount Dillingham".

She knocked and, because she felt that the man who had watched her up the stairs was perhaps listening, she made it a very tentative sound.

There was no answer and after a moment she knocked again and then realising there was a handle on the door, she turned it.

The door opened.

She found herself in a small narrow passage with two doors at the other end of it.

"Charles!"

It was hardly a call because by now she was shaking.

"Who is it?" her brother's voice replied.

A door was opened and she saw Charles wearing only a shirt and trousers.

"Good God Orissa!" he exclaimed. "What are you doing here?"

"I had to come, Charles," Orissa answered. "She turned me out and I cannot get back into the house tonight."

There was no need for her to explain who 'She' was.

"Dammit!" Charles ejaculated. "This is too much! Why do you put up with it?"

"What else can I do?"

He saw she was shivering.

"Come and sit by the fire," he suggested.

"You ought not to have come here."

"I have nowhere else to go," Orissa answered simply.

She crossed the Bed-room as she spoke and sat down on the hearth-rug in front of the fire holding out her cold hands to the warm flames.

"Do you mean 'She' really threw you out of the house?" Charles asked almost incredulously as he followed her across the room.

"With some violence," Orissa replied. "If my hair was not so thick I should have bruises on my head."

As she spoke there was a little smile on her lips. It was such a relief to be here with her brother that now everything which had happened seemed almost amusing rather than tragic.

"Oh, God!" Charles exclaimed. "Why did the old man ever get himself mixed up with a woman like that?"

"I have been asking myself the same question for eight years," Orissa said. "When I think how lovely and gentle Mama was . . ."

She stopped in the middle of the sentence.

After all this time it was still difficult to speak of her mother without feeling near to tears.

"I know," Charles said sympathetically,

sitting down in an arm-chair beside the fire, "but you cannot go on like this."

"Next time it happens you may not be here," Orissa replied.

"You ought not to be here now," Charles said. "I hope no-one saw you arrive."

Orissa hesitated.

She did not wish to tell him the truth because it might upset him. At the same time she never lied to her brother.

"As a matter of fact there was . . . someone on the . . . first floor," she answered, "a tall man with grey eyes."

"Hell!"

Orissa looked at him and he said:

"It could not be worse! That must have been Meredith."

"I am . . . sorry," Orissa faltered. "Does it matter . . . very much?"

"It will not help things," Charles answered.

"Why not? Who is he?"

"He is Major the Honourable Myron Meredith," Charles informed her, "and I am in his black books already."

"Why?" Orissa enquired, "and even if he is Major, why has he got authority over you?"

"Because he is not an ordinary Major," Charles answered. "He has a kind of roving commission. If you ask me, he is Secret Intelligence or something of the sort. Anyway, he is quite a big-wig in India."

"And why should you be in his black books?" Orissa enquired with an almost fierce note in her voice.

"I have been in a spot of trouble already," Charles admitted.

"What sort of trouble?"

"You are too inquisitive," he replied, "but I do not mind telling you she was very pretty!"

"Oh, a woman!"

"Is it not always a woman?" Charles demanded.

"Why should that concern Major Meredith?"

"Only because she happened to be a brother Officer's wife! He spoke at some length on 'the Honour of the Regiment' our prestige in India and all that sort of thing!"

"But is Major Meredith in our Regiment?" Orissa asked.

The Royal Chilterns had been the family Regiment of the Fanes and the Hobarts for generations. Son had followed father and grandfather until they all spoke of it with a possessive affection.

"No — thank goodness!" Charles replied. "He is attached to the Bengal Lancers, but

24

is always at Staff Headquarters. I wish he would stay there! If he had not been so blasted snoopy, neither he nor anyone else would have found out about my little escapade."

"What was that?"

"Oh, a trip to the Hills when I thought we had covered our tracks very successfully! But trust Meredith to be everywhere he is not wanted!"

Thinking of those searching, grey eyes she had encountered on the stairs, Orissa could believe this to be true.

"As a matter of fact I hate him," Charles went on. "It is, I am confident, entirely due to him that Gerald Dewar shot himself!"

Orissa turned her head sharply.

"Shot himself?" she repeated. "But why?"

"That is what I would like to know," Charles replied almost savagely. "Gerald was my best friend. A nicer chap you could not imagine. But he got mixed up with a woman when he was on leave in Simla. Dammed attractive she was too!"

"But why should Major Meredith interfere?" Orissa asked.

"That is a question I wanted to ask him myself," Charles replied, "but I could not pluck up courage. Anyway, Gerald shot himself and we were all told it was a regrettable accident. Not that I — for one — believed that!"

"What can Major Meredith do about my . . . coming here?" Orissa asked in a low voice.

"Only make trouble because I have more or less promised to behave myself with regard to the fair sex," Charles replied.

He paused and added with a smile:

"Only 'more or less'! But that certainly does not permit me to entertain a woman in Army lodgings."

"Surely you can tell him I am your sister," Orissa suggested.

"Do you think that will make it any better?" Charles asked. "I should then have to explain that my sister had been thrown out of her home in the middle of the night and had nowhere to go."

His voice was angry as he went on:

"I am damned if I will let anyone know the sort of condition my father is in now! He was greatly respected by everyone when he commanded the Regiment. You know that as well as I do."

"I remember how proud Mama always was of him," Orissa said softly.

"That is why Meredith can think what he likes," Charles said firmly. "After all I am not the only officer who likes the company of the female sex. And if they run after me, even to the extent of coming here, how can I stop them?"

"I am sure you would not!" Orissa exclaimed and they both laughed.

Charles had always been gay and irresponsible, she thought, and it would be impossible for anyone — even Major Meredith — to expect him to live a monastic life however much he might preach propriety to him.

As they sat laughing together, a stranger would have been unable to find any resemblance between brother and sister.

The Fanes all through the centuries — and it was a very ancient family — had always been either very fair or very dark.

The dark Fanes had first come into the family in the reign of Charles II when an ancestor had brought home from Cadiz a black haired, magnolia-skinned Senorita, and their children had taken after her.

Charles was a fair Fane with blue eyes and fair curly hair which, combined with handsome features, made him irresistible to women.

Orissa on the other hand resembled her Spanish ancestress.

She had long dark hair with blue lights in it which grew in a small widow's peak on her oval forehead. Her eyes, were enormous and seemed at times, when she was worried or angry, almost purple in their depths. Her skin was like a magnolia blossom. She was also small-boned and had a grace that was almost indescribable.

Anything that Orissa wore seemed to mould itself to her exquisite figure and to achieve an elegance which made other women in her company appear clumsy and overdressed.

Now looking at her seated on the hearth-rug, her small head shining in the light from the flames and her skin almost dazzlingly white against the red of her gown, her brother said:

"I have to do something about you, Orissa."

"I am waiting to hear your suggestions," she answered.

"We must have some relations."

"Not many," Orissa replied, "and those there are, Papa — or rather 'She' — has quarrelled with. They never come near us now."

"If only Mama's parents were not dead."

"Or if Uncle Henry were in England!" Orissa sighed.

"Uncle Henry!" Charles exclaimed. "That of course is the solution!"

"What do you mean?"

"You must go to him. After all he is a bachelor. You could make yourself useful and I believe he would like to have you with him?"

"Do you mean in India?" Orissa asked incredulously.

"Of course," Charles replied.

He saw the sudden light which seemed to illuminate her whole face.

"Oh, Charles, if only I could!"

"Why not?" he asked.

"Do you really think that Uncle Henry would let me live with him?"

"I have only just thought of it this moment," Charles admitted, "but I see no reason why not. He has always been fond of you. He always asks if I have heard from you, and now you are grown up it would be quite different from saddling him with a child."

"To be in India again would be Heaven," Orissa said almost beneath her breath. "I dream of it every night!"

"Does it really mean so much to you?" Charles asked curiously.

"It is the only home I have ever known," Orissa answered, "and I was happy . . . unbelievably happy until Mama died."

"Then somehow we must get you to

Uncle Henry. Let me see — he was in Delhi when I left and the Regiment is likely to be there for another month or so."

Orissa's eyes were shining as she said:

"But I will have to write to him. It will take some time to get a reply. What shall I do in the meantime?"

Charles did not answer for a moment and Orissa knew he was thinking. Then he said:

"I have an idea!"

"What is it?"

"To tell the truth I was wondering just now how I was going to raise your fare. I am badly dipped at the moment."

"Pretty ladies are . . . I understand . . . very expensive," Orissa teased.

"You are right there," Charles confessed. "So quite frankly, although I suppose I could borrow it from somewhere, it would be very difficult unless you agree to another suggestion."

"What is that?" Orissa asked.

"I was in the office this morning taking instructions about our classes for tomorrow when General Sir Arthur Critchley came in. He is the General Officer Commanding, Bombay."

Orissa did not speak but her eyes were watching her brother's face intently.

"The General asked the Adjutant,"

Charles went on, "if he knew of any officers' wives who were travelling out on the *Dorunda.*"

" 'No, Sir' the Adjutant answered.

" 'I have to find someone', the General went on, 'who will look after my small grandson during the voyage. A cousin was coming with us, but unfortunately she has had an accident and has cancelled her trip at the last moment.'

" 'Sorry to hear that, Sir', the Adjutant remarked.

" 'It is a cursed nuisance,' the General said. 'I cannot expect my wife to be responsible for a child of five during the whole voyage. It would be too much for her.'

" 'No, Sir'.

" 'And there is not much point in taking out a Nanny when my daughter-in-law has an Ayah waiting in Bombay.'

" 'No, Sir, I can see that,' the Adjutant agreed.

" 'Perhaps you had better get on to the Shipping Line for me,' the General said. 'See if there is a lady travelling to India who would look after the child in return for her First Class Fare. I am quite willing to pay that — one way, of course!'

" 'I understand, Sir,' the Adjutant answered."

31

Charles stopped speaking. Orissa looked at him and exclaimed excitedly:

"And you think I might go? But supposing they have found someone already?"

"They will not have done that," Charles answered.

"How do you know?" Orissa asked.

Her brother grinned at her.

"The Adjutant told me to find Hughes, who is a newly-joined Lieutenant, and tell him to get on to the Shipping Line. As I was in a hurry I forgot all about it!"

"Oh, Charles!" Orissa exclaimed. "That is just like you!"

"If you ask me, it is fate!" Charles said positively.

"It does seem like it," Orissa agreed, "and how are you going to introduce me?"

Charles thought for a moment.

"I can tell you one thing," he said at length. "I know Lady Critchley. She will not want to chaperon a young unmarried girl. She has always set her face against it, even in Bombay. She thinks they are a nuisance hanging around the Subalterns, and makes disparaging remarks about those who come out to India merely with the hope of getting married."

Orissa looked dismayed.

"Then she will not want me."

"Not — if she thinks you are unmarried!"

Orissa looked at him quickly.

"You mean I could pretend to be married?" she questioned.

"Why not?" her brother asked. "After all, if people know who you are, they will think it very strange that you are going out to India alone. They would certainly expect you to have a Chaperon on the voyage and there would be a lot of explaining to do."

He smiled.

"If you simply turn up as Mrs. Something or other and take charge of the child, who is going to argue or ask questions?"

"No, of course not," Orissa cried. "Oh, Charles, you are brilliant!"

"I always thought I had a brain hidden away somewhere," her brother said modestly. "As a matter of fact I am quite certain my report on this course will be as good, if not better, than the others get."

"I am sure you will top them all," Orissa said. "Now what am I to do?"

"First of all, we have to find you a name and a wedding-ring."

"I have Mama's ring. And who is my husband supposed to be?"

"Say he is in the East India Company," her brother answered. "That covers a pretty wide field — and you should call yourself something quite ordinary, like Smith or Brown."

"I refuse!" Orissa protested. "I could not bear to have such an uninteresting name."

"Well, anything but Fane," Charles acceded.

"Then I will be Lane — Mrs. Lane," Orissa decided. "It is always wise to have a name as much like one's own as possible, and Mrs. Lane, wife of a gentleman in the East India Company sounds eminently respectable."

"What I will do first thing tomorrow morning," Charles said, "is to tell the Adjutant to inform Lady Critchley that he has found exactly the right person to look after her grandchild. They will not be able to see you until you are on board as there is so little time before the ship sails the day after tomorrow."

"So soon!" Orissa exclaimed, but she was not complaining.

"I will give you your fare to Tilbury," Charles continued, "and all you have to do is get yourself there. The Adjutant will tell the Ship's Agents that you are to be one of the passengers and of course the General will arrange the cabin and all that sort of thing."

"Oh, Charles, it is all too wonderful to be

true!" Orissa cried.

"It certainly solves your problem," her brother said with satisfaction.

"I hate to mention it," Orissa said, "but I shall have to have some money. After all there will be the train fare from Bombay to Delhi. I don't suppose the General will pay that."

"He will not pay a penny more than he has to — you can be sure of that!" Charles answered, "I will let you have what I can. But, as I have already told you, it is not easy at the moment."

"I hate to be a drag on you," Orissa said softly.

"To tell the truth," Charles replied, "I am feeling rather guilty that I have not done something about you before. I knew things were bad at home, but not as bad as they are."

"It does not matter now. Nothing matters!" Orissa smiled, "as long as I can get away, and be with Uncle Henry and in India!"

Her brother, seeing her face radiant in the light of the flames, thought that she was unlikely to be on her Uncle's hands for long. He had not seen his sister for two years and he was astounded by the difference those years had made.

From being rather a thin, scraggy little girl she had grown into a strangely beautiful young woman.

She was not, he thought, like anyone else he had ever seen, and there was in fact something almost Eastern in the darkness of her hair and the mystery of her huge eyes.

"Do you know, Orissa," he said following the train of his thoughts, "you might almost pass as a Rajput Princess."

"You could not pay me a bigger compliment," Orissa answered. "In my dreams I am always a part of India. I never belonged to the cold and misery that I have found here."

She paused and added:

"England has never been home to me. Home was being with Mama."

"And so when you talk of going home you mean India?"

"When I return to India I shall be home."

Charles laughed affectionately.

"Well, as long as you are happy I will be able to go off to Egypt with a clear conscience."

Orissa gave a quick sigh as if she just remembered the danger he would be in.

"If only you were coming with me."

"I do not suppose it will be long before I am back with the Regiment," Charles answered. "We have sent an Indian force to Egypt. They should be disembarking now at Port Said. I shall join up with them as soon as I arrive."

There was an enthusiasm in his voice which told Orissa he was looking forward to what lay ahead.

Charles had always loved his Regimental duties and had always been a success.

He was six years older than she was and she had adored him ever since she had been a small child.

She had not even been jealous that her mother had undoubtedly loved Charles more than she had loved her.

Orissa had understood. Charles had been the first, the only son, and there was between mother and son a closeness, an indefinable link that there could never be between mother and daughter.

Yet she had adored her beautiful and gentle mother and it had been a tragedy beyond words when she had died of cholera because she would tend the small children of one of their native servants.

Even now Orissa could not bear the memory of the small white coffin being carried from their house in Delhi through the streets and into the churchyard. It did not seem real, but an evil dream from which she must wake and find it was all untrue.

But instead there had been the long voyage home; the agony of saying good-bye to everything she had loved and which had seemed an indivisible part of herself.

"What a very unattractive child!" she had heard someone say to the Colonel's wife on board the ship taking her to England. "It seems strange when her mother was so pretty."

"Plain children often turn into pretty women," the Colonel's wife had replied.

Orissa had often remembered those words. Because the beauty of India was steeped deep into her soul, she had resented her own plainness.

She had not realised then that much of it was because after her mother's death she had forgotten how to smile, and more often than not she looked at people with a scowl on her face.

There was little to make her smile or feel happy after her father re-married, and yet gradually, because youth is resilient, she learned to find in little things, the beauty for which she hungered.

A mass of golden flowers being sold in a florist-shop would remind her of the marigolds that were made into garlands in India, and for a moment their vivid colour seemed like a ray of happiness in the darkness of her despair.

She would watch for the blossoms of spring, and the small white petals of the fruit trees would make her think of the pure loveliness of a lotus flower opening in their garden.

Sometimes in summer she would listen to the song of the English birds and imagine it was the noisy chatter, cawings and flutter of wings among the orange trees as dawn broke, vivid in the Indian sky.

"What is the matter with you?" her Stepmother once had asked Orissa savagely and Orissa answered truthfully:

"I am home-sick."

It was not surprising that the Countess had not understood.

"Oh, Charles! Charles!" Orissa cried now, "how can I ever thank you? I might have known you would not fail me."

"You will have to act your part well," Charles answered. "I shall be in a worse mess than usual if the General discovers who you are."

"Suppose later I visit Bombay with Uncle Henry?"

"It is not likely as the Regiment is always in the North," Charles said confidently.

"But if you do, just keep out of the General's way!"

"I will try."

"And now, for Heaven's sake," Charles begged, "do not give me any more problems to solve. I am worn out with thinking about them. What we have to decide now is where you are to sleep tonight."

"I could go to an Hotel," Orissa said doubtfully.

"What decent Hotel would take in a young woman at this time of night without even a piece of luggage?" he asked.

Orissa smiled at him.

"Then I shall have to stay here."

"I suppose so, but let us hope that Meredith does not get to hear about it. He will think the worst — and let him think it! But I do not want to have to make explanations to anyone. I only pray that most of them do not realise that Father is alive."

"They must not see him now," Orissa said quickly. "They must remember him as he was . . . as we remember him when we were young."

"And that is why you have to be clever," Charles said sharply. "You will be Mrs. Lane or whatever you call yourself, until you get to Bombay. Then vanish!"

"I will do that," Orissa promised, "and

thank you, darling Charles! You are the most wonderful brother anyone could ever have!"

"I must say I think I am rather clever!" Viscount Dillingham said with some satisfaction.

Chapter Two

Orissa moved quietly about the cabin so as not to disturb the sleeping child.

He had been excited during the railway journey to Tilbury, and when his grandmother brought him on board he ran wildly about the ship thrilled by everything he saw.

Orissa had taken the precaution of leaving London on an earlier train so that she would not encounter the General and his wife until they were on board the *Dorunda*.

Charles of course had not been able to see her off for fear someone should recognise him at the Station.

But he had collected her in a cab from Eaton Place and set her down at Waterloo.

"You cannot get into much trouble," he said, "if you walk straight to the waiting train."

Orissa laughed.

"Have you forgotten I am a married

woman, quite competent to look after my-self?"

"If I were not certain that Lady Critchley is a dragon who will keep all prospective suitors well away, I should be worried about you on the voyage," Charles said.

"Do not worry," Orissa begged, "and take care of yourself, dearest. I shall be thinking of you and praying you will be safe."

She had kissed her brother good-bye and stepped out of the cab with a sense of adventure lighting her eyes and making her feel as if she walked on air.

She could hardly believe it was true! All the obstacles seemed to have dispersed and she was really starting on her journey to India.

There had, as it happened, been quite a number of things to worry about.

The first had been getting away from Charles's lodgings early in the morning.

After quite a fierce argument, Orissa had insisted on sleeping on the sofa while Charles occupied the bed.

"You are too big for the sofa, while for me it will be quite comfortable," she said. "Besides, I can hardly undress if I have nothing else to put on!"

Charles had finally given way and with several blankets and an eiderdown on top of her, which Charles said scornfully he never used, she was warm and slept quite well.

Charles had fortunately told his servant to call him at 6 o'clock as he was going riding before he went to the Barracks.

The man was considerably surprised when he entered the small Sitting-room which adjoined the Bed-room to find Orissa curled up on the sofa.

"We have to get my sister out of the place without her being seen, Dawkins," Charles told him.

"That'll be easy, Sir," Dawkins replied. "Her Ladyship can go out the back way."

Dawkins paused and looking at Orissa's evening gown, observed:

"It's real cold this morning, M'Lady."

"What can I find you to wear?" Charles asked, now that his sister's inadequate clothing had been brought to his attention.

Orissa looked round helpless. It was Dawkins who solved the problem.

He took down one of the velvet curtains in the Sitting-room, cut off the brass rings, and Orissa found it made her quite an adequate cloak.

"I'll fetch it back, M'Lady, when the Captain can spare me. We mustn't dispose of Government property."

"Certainly not!" Orissa smiled. "And

thank you."

She felt quite warm and not so conspicuous with a cloak over her gown.

It was agreed that Dawkins should find a Hackney carriage and bring it to the back of the building.

"You'll be able to see when I've got one, M'Lady, if you look out of the window of the Bed-room," Dawkins said to Orissa. "All you've got to do then is to come downstairs, turn sharp left when you reach the bottom and you'll find a door straight ahead of you."

Orissa had therefore watched as instructed and although it had taken Dawkins some time so early in the morning to find a Hackney cab, she had finally seen one draw up outside.

Saying good-bye to her brother she hurried downstairs.

The gas-lights had been extinguished and as there was still very little light outside, the stairs were dark. So she held tightly on to the bannisters in case she should trip.

The place seemed very quiet. It was only when she reached the first floor that one of the doors opened and a man emerged.

With a frightened leap of her heart, Orissa knew it was Major Meredith.

It was too late for her to go back up the stairs again, and the only thing was to hurry past hoping he would not see her face.

At the same time she could not help glancing at him, and she thought that even in the half-light she could distinguish a look of contempt in his eyes.

She ran on and hurried down the next flight of stairs with a speed that made it appear that all the hounds of hell were at her heels.

She found the back door which Dawkins had described to her and the safety of the Hackney cab.

She did not tell Charles what had happened because she could not bear to upset him the last few moments of their time together.

He had said that he might come and see her that evening, but instead he had sent her a note to say he was unable to do so, but that everything had worked out splendidly.

"Lady Critchley," he wrote, "is delighted that a Mrs. Lane will look after her grandchild on their journey to India!"

Charles had however arrived the following morning, by which time Orissa had packed her trunks and broken the news both to her father and Step-mother that she was leaving.

She had thought when she returned the

previous day that the Countess was slightly shame-faced, feeling perhaps that in turning Orissa out of the house, she had for once gone too far.

They neither of them referred to the fact that Orissa had been away all night, but it was obvious that the Countess was on the defensive when Charles arrived.

"I should have thought that it would have been polite," she said accusingly, "to have asked your father's and my permission before arranging for Orissa to live with her Uncle."

Charles had looked with disgust at the fat, blowzy woman who bore his father's name.

"Obviously she cannot stay here and suffer from the manner in which you behaved to her the night before last," he answered.

"I've done my best for your sister," the Countess retorted angrily. "If she's been telling you tales about me, I can assure you they're untrue!"

Charles had not deigned to reply and the Countess had continued beligerently:

"I've a good mind to prevent Orissa leaving. Her father is her Guardian, not you, and if he tells her to stay, she'll have to obey him."

"I can assure you of one thing," Charles said, "that I would not permit Orissa to remain under this roof any longer whatever you might say or do."

He had walked away from the Countess to find his father in the small Sitting-room at the back of the house where he sat and drank.

For once the Earl was comparatively sober and when he said good-bye Orissa felt he was genuinely sorry to lose her.

Because he felt generous, or perhaps because he was ashamed of his wife's behaviour, he gave Orissa five pounds. This she accepted gratefully.

Charles had sent her twenty pounds the day before with his note and she had, although she felt it was wrong to do so, expended a few pounds in buying materials to make herself some dresses.

They were pretty muslins and they had been very cheap. She had felt she could not arrive in India almost in rags, and she certainly did not wish her Uncle to feel embarrassed at her shabby appearance.

Colonel Hobart was well off and Orissa was certain that he would, in his usual generous manner, provide her with enough money to buy herself clothes once she was living in his house. But in the meantime, she was ashamed of her wardrobe.

Everything in it she had made herself and

apart from one evening gown which was only six months old she had bought nothing new for two or three years.

It was amazing however, she thought, what one could do with a few yards of ribbon and some lengths of tulle, combined with the fact that she was extremely skilful with her needle.

When she received her father's gift, she was thankful that she had been a little extravagant in buying the few things she had!

It would give her something to do aboard ship, and the brightly coloured muslins were eminently suitable for the heat of India.

Her travelling outfit, a woollen dress of deep blue with a cloak to match was old. Orissa thought it was almost thread-bare and did not realise that anyone looking at her would see only the brightness of her eyes, the happiness of her smile and the perfect magnolia whiteness of her skin.

"Take care of yourself," Charles said, as standing in the station she gave him a last wave of her hand and she turned and followed a porter who had put her baggage on a truck.

Then to the cab-driver he said:

"Take me to Wellington Barracks."

As the cab drove away his thoughts were

of himself and the journey he in his turn would be undertaking within a few days.

It was only when she had gone on board that Orissa remembered she had not reminded Charles to send a telegram to her Uncle after the ship sailed.

They had agreed that it would be a mistake to dispatch one before she had actually left England in case Colonel Hobart made objections or tried to postpone her visit.

"Once you are on the high seas he can do nothing," Charles said confidently.

"You really think he will want me?" Orissa asked nervously.

She was suddenly afraid that she was being presumptuous in assuming that her Uncle would welcome her company.

"I know he will!" Charles answered. "At the same time we will take no chances. I will send him a telegram after you have left."

They had not spoken of it again and Orissa had meant to remind him, but she was sure there was no need.

Charles, despite his proverbial bad memory, could not forget anything so important!

Then she forgot her worries, anxieties and everything else in the joy of knowing that the great adventure had begun.

She took care to look demure, and she

hoped, very respectable when the General and Lady Critchley came on board, and a Steward was sent to bring her to their cabin.

The black-hulled *Dorunda* a full-rigged, four-masted, screw-propelled ship was one of the latest vessels on the run to India.

Orissa had hardly been on board for ten minutes before a Steward explained with pride that the engines were of a novel and exceptionally economical type and that her full boiler-power drove her at 15.31 knots in her trial runs in the Clyde.

What Orissa found more interesting were the passenger arrangements which were quite different from those on the ship in which she had travelled back from India six years earlier.

In the long covered space under the spar-deck there were on each side two rows of First Class cabins with berths for ninety-five passengers.

The State-rooms, of which she and her charge occupied one, were fitted so that the upper berths folded out of the way and the lower berths divided into two, sliding aside into seats so that a table could be placed between them.

In this way a cabin which measured 9' × 6' could become a Sitting-room in the day time.

The public Saloons were very spacious and impressive extending from side to side of the Citadel house.

"There are sufficient centre and side-tables in the Dining-Saloon," a Steward told Orissa proudly, "to dine one hundred passengers!"

What was far more sensational was that the ship was lit at night by incandescent electric lights! Besides this wonder there was an organ, an excellent piano and, what delighted Orissa, an elegantly carved book-case containing three hundred volumes.

She did not see the Second Class accommodation nor that of the Third Class, but she was told they were unusually comfortable.

"It is a very big ship," little Neil kept saying to her after she had taken him into her charge. And she had to agree that it was indeed a big ship, the biggest she had ever seen.

The General, as might be expected, was obviously a military man, lean, wiry, with a skin like leather.

He had a commanding manner, so that Orissa thought that even when he was trying to be pleasant he addressed her rather as if he was ordering about a new recruit.

Lady Critchley was in fact far more awe-inspiring.

She was a cold, severe type of woman who must have been extremely handsome in her youth. But the Indian climate had taken its toll of her complexion, and although she could not have been much over fifty, her hair was dead-white.

It seemed to Orissa strange that Neil who looked fragile should be going back to India, until his grandmother explained:

"The child is delicate, and we thought as the Indian climate seemed bad for him he would improve in health if we sent him home."

She looked at her grandson as she spoke and there was a look of displeasure in her eyes as she continued:

"He has however pined continually for his mother, and my sister with whom he was staying felt the only solution was for him to return to her."

"I can understand his wanting to be with his own family," Orissa said softly, thinking of herself and her own misery at being sent to England.

"It is exceedingly tiresome and a worry for my daughter," Lady Critchley said. "She had two other small children. Fortunately her husband will now be in Bombay for some months. The climate there is not so oppressive."

She had not thanked Orissa for undertaking the task of looking after little Neil but merely inferred she was lucky to have her fare paid, a sentiment with which she was quite prepared to agree.

But she could see that Charles had been right in saying that Lady Critchley would have been extremely annoyed if she had been expected to chaperon Lady Orissa Fane rather than give orders to the quiet, sub-servient Mrs. Lane.

There were the usual dramas before the ship sailed, including passionate good-byes from those who were being left behind; a great deal of confusion over lost luggage; stewards being shouted for and sailors hurrying in all directions.

Standing at the rail on the First Class deck to watch the late arrivals come on board, Orissa noticed there was quite a number of soldiers climbing up the gang-way onto the Third Class deck, their kit-bags hunched on their shoulders.

They were leaving some very tearful wives or sweethearts on the quay, and handkerchiefs were already wiping streaming eyes as a Band played and the non-travellers who had come aboard were asked to go ashore.

Unfortunately Orissa could not wait for the last moment to see the ship pull away from the quay.

It was very cold, it had also begun to rain and she felt sure that Neil should be kept in the warm.

Accordingly she took him to their cabin and tried to watch through a port-hole.

They were however on the wrong side of the ship to see very much, but when finally Orissa felt the engines start up and heard the sails being set, she knew she was saying good-bye to England.

She hoped it was for a very long time.

A Steward brought some tea to the cabin, but Neil was too tired to eat the elegant sandwiches or even the cream cakes. He drank a little milk and Orissa realised his head was nodding.

The State-room contained four berths but there would be no necessity to use the upper ones as there were only the two of them, in the cabin.

She rang for the steward and had Neil's bunk made up. Then she unpacked her own things and as she put them away in the cupboards and the deep drawers she realised with satisfaction that she would have plenty of room on the voyage.

The General and Lady Critchley were

next door, but when they came to say good-night to their grandchild, he was already fast asleep.

"I am glad you have put him to bed, Mrs. Lane," Lady Critchley said to Orissa with just a hint of approval in her tone.

"There was one thing I wanted to ask you," Orissa said, "would you wish me to have supper here in the cabin or downstairs in the Dining-Hall?"

Lady Critchley hesitated before she said:

"You will of course dine at our table, Mrs. Lane. You are after all obliging us by looking after Neil on the voyage. You are hardly in the same category as a Governess."

It seemed to Orissa that her Ladyship was convincing herself of what was the right thing and in actual fact being extremely magnanimous to the woman she thought was only the wife of a petty official.

"Thank you," Orissa said.

"You will of course ask the Steward to keep an eye on Neil while you are downstairs," Lady Critchley went on. "But I understand from my sister that, whilst he is nervous and excitable in the daytime, he seldom has disturbed nights."

When she had finished speaking, Lady Critchley swept back to her own cabin and Orissa with a little smile closed the door behind her.

It was quite obvious that Lady Critchley was being condescendingly kindly to the little nobody who was obliging her by acting as a nurse-maid.

She wondered what Her Ladyship's attitude would be if she knew her real identity. Then she remembered that Charles had told her on no account to let anyone find out.

'He has been so angelic to me,' Orissa told herself, 'I must be very careful indeed.'

The Steward told her that dinner was to be later than usual the first night at sea.

"Takes time for the Chefs to get themselves organised," he said, "but you'll get good food on this ship. D'you know, Ma'am, the refrigeration chambers hold five hundred tons of meat and there's an additional compartment that'll hold five hundred tons more!"

"Good gracious!" Orissa exclaimed. "It sounds horrifying that we could possibly eat so much!"

"Well, it all depends on the weather, Ma'am," the Steward said with a grin. "People who get sea-sick aren't hungry!"

He picked up the tea-tray and added:

"But Ma'am you'll enjoy yourself tonight."

Orissa changed into her best evening gown. Somewhere she remembered someone saying:

"First impressions are always important. People get a fixed idea of you in their minds and seldom change it."

The gown, which was of peacock blue, had been a remnant that she could just afford at a sale in one of the big shops in Kensington. She had wanted it because it had reminded her of the lovely blue mosaics which decorated the mosques in India.

She had made it very simply with a huge bow as a bustle at the back, but because she had been rather short of material it clung tightly over her figure in the front revealing the smallness of her waist and the soft swelling of her breasts.

She felt a little self-conscious when she was finally ready to go down to dinner wondering whether Lady Critchley would think she was too smart or perhaps too dashing for her humble position.

But the alternative was either the red dress she had worn the night her Step-mother had thrown her out into the snow and which had stains on it which she had not yet had time to remove, or a green gown.

It was for this garment which was some years old, that she had bought the tulle and silk ribbons which she believed would transform it into something a little more stylish than it was at the moment.

The ship was very warm, but just in case she felt cold Orissa carried over her arm a scarf which had once belonged to her mother.

It was Indian and had silver paillettes sewn on to a thin net which sparkled and glittered with every movement.

She had arranged her black hair close to her head and holding herself superbly, with a little extra pride because she was nervous, she went from her cabin to the Saloon.

She had heard the General and Lady Critchley leave their cabin some minutes earlier and she found them as she expected in the large comfortable Saloon already holding court.

Shyly Orissa hovered on the outside of the circle when the General noticed her.

"Ah — Mrs. Lane, here you are," he said ponderously. "I think it is time we went down to dinner."

"The gong sounded some moments ago," Lady Critchley said with a glance at Orissa to suggest that she was late.

Then like a ship in full sail she led the way down the stairs to the Dining-Saloon.

As it was the first night at sea everybody was in good humour.

There was the sound of popping champagne corks, and it seemed to Orissa as if everyone was talking at the tops of their voices in case they should not be heard above the noise of the engines.

She had expected the General and Lady Critchley to have a table to themselves, but it appeared that as the most important people on board, they were seated in the place of honour at the Captain's table.

Tonight the Captain was not present as he was on the bridge taking the ship out to sea and there were a number of empty seats.

But there were a Colonel Onslow and his wife travelling to Alexandria and another Colonel who was joining the Nile Expedition at Port Said and lastly two couples of lesser Military importance who were en route to Bombay.

Lady Critchley was on the right of the Captain's empty chair with the General next to her. Orissa sat on his right.

"Do you know India well, Mrs. Lane?" he boomed.

"I have not been there for some years," she replied.

"Your husband is newly appointed then," the General said. "I imagine he has gone ahead to get things ready for you."

"Yes, that is right," Orissa agreed.

The General having been conversationally

polite then started a discussion with the Colonel travelling to Alexandria and the other officer journeying to Port Said.

They were all, Orissa found, of the opinion that the Prime Minister, Mr. Gladstone, had been extremely tardy in waiting so long to dispatch an Army to relieve General Gordon.

"I can only hope they will not be too late," the General said gloomily.

"I understand," Colonel Onslow answered, "that General Gordon's force in Khartoum consists of only two thousand Turks and six hundred black troops, while the Mahdi's Army is estimated at fifteen to twenty thousand."

"If Wolseley gets there in time," the General said, "he will easily disperse an Army of untrained, undisciplined natives."

"I believe they are having trouble in passing the Cataracts," Lady Critchley remarked.

"They are," Colonel McDougal replied. "Even so I cannot really see why it should have taken as long as it has."

Orissa was extremely interested.

Her Uncle had known General Gordon well and often talked of his fantastic personality, his brilliance and his eccentricity.

Gordon's successes in China, where he

proved himself one of the greatest Commanders of Irregulars of all time, had made him a legend in his lifetime.

When after much hesitation and the toss of a coin he agreed to become Governor General of the Sudan he wrote:

"I go up alone, with an infinite Almighty God to direct and guide me."

Then when a Fakir called the Mahdi "the expected one" had declared a Holy War and overrun a vast amount of territory, Gordon was sent back to Khartoum with the main object of effecting the vacuation of the Egyptian Troops.

But in March 1884 the Mahdi's huge army of Dervishes had closed round Khartoum and besieged it.

It was not until August that the unceasing pressure of public opinion, supported in private by the Queen, compelled the Government to agree that steps should be taken to relieve the beleaguered town.

On her way down from London in the train Orissa had bought "*The Graphic*" magazine and studied a picture of the Guards Division of the Camel Corps crossing the Bayunda desert on their way to Khartoum.

They were commanded by Sir Charles Wilson and Major Kitchener and she found herself praying for her brother's sake, if for no other reason, that they might reach General Gordon in time.

The *"Graphic"* of the second week in January had also had some information about India describing the celebrations which had taken place when the new Viceroy, Lord Dufferin, had arrived in Bombay to succeed Lord Rippon. It had gone on to speak of trouble on the North-West Frontier.

This was something which Orissa had heard talked of incessantly in the past, because her father's Regiment was nearly always stationed in the Northern Provinces.

She longed now to ask the General what the situation had been like when he was last in India, but she felt that it might be unwise to show too obvious a knowledge of Army matters.

At the same time she felt certain that sooner or later the conversation would turn from the Nile Expedition to the trouble in Afghanistan.

Dinner was, as the Steward predicted, extremely good and when it was finished Lady Critchley announced:

"We will have coffee in the Saloon."

She left the table having first invited Colonel Onslow and his wife to join them and also Colonel McDougal.

She very pointedly ignored the other people at the Captain's table, and Orissa following in the wake of Lady Critchley's rustling grey bustle felt rather sorry for them.

She knew how snobby the English were in India and felt their fellow passengers would be longing on their arrival to tell their friends how intimate they had been with the G.O.C. Bombay and his wife, that is, if they ever got on such terms!

Coffee was brought by an attentive Steward and the General ordered brandy for himself and the two Colonels.

Orissa had decided that as soon as she finished her coffee she would be expected to retire to her cabin.

She was just about to rise to her feet when she heard the General say:

"Hello, Meredith, I heard you were on board. I was expecting to see you at dinner!"

It was with the greatest difficulty Orissa prevented herself from starting violently.

At the same time she thought that her heart had stopped beating as with deliberate slowness she turned her head to see standing by their table the man she had last seen on the stairs of Charles's lodgings.

Major Meredith looked, she thought, even

more formidable than he had in the dimness of the ill lit landing when she had slipped past him to run down the stairs.

Then she told herself there was no need to panic.

It had been very dark and, while she knew who he was because Charles had talked about him, why should he connect her in any way with the woman he was now about to meet in the company of the G.O.C. Bombay?

Major Meredith shook hands with the General and then walked around the table to Lady Critchley.

"How nice to see you, Major," she said in her usual cold voice. "I do not know whether you have met Colonel and Mrs. Onslow who are travelling to Alexandria?"

Major Meredith shook them both by the hand and was then introduced to Colonel McDougal.

It gave Orissa time to convince herself that, if she only kept her head and behaved quite ordinarily, Major Meredith would not recognise her.

"And this is Mrs. Lane," Lady Critchley said almost as if it was an after-thought, "who is travelling to India and has very kindly consented to look after little Neil, my daughter's child, whom we are taking back with us to Bombay."

Orissa bowed her head but did not attempt to put out her hand. Major Meredith bowed in response.

His face was quite expressionless. There was not the slightest gleam of recognition in his grey eyes.

'I was right!' Orissa thought elatedly. 'He has not recognised me!'

"Sit down, Meredith," the General commanded, "and tell me the latest news from Khartoum."

"There was none when I left London," the Major replied.

He had a very strange voice, Orissa decided. It was different from any other man's.

It was very deep. It seemed too to have a resonance that awoke some chord of memory which she could not quite place and then she told herself she was being imaginative.

"And what news from India?" Lady Critchley asked. "We seem to be out of touch ever since we have been home."

"That is what we all feel when we are away," Major Meredith replied.

"I see there is more trouble on the Frontier," Colonel Onslow remarked.

Major Meredith smiled.

"Is there ever anything else?"

"But they say that Russia is only waiting for a suitable moment to march into Afghanistan and capture Herat."

"We cannot allow that!" the General said positively.

"Of course not, Sir," Major Meredith agreed.

"I thought we had settled the trouble with Afghanistan several years ago," Mrs. Onslow remarked plaintively. "I cannot understand why we must have one alarm after another."

"I will explain it quite simply," Major Meredith answered. "In the North West the savage, aggressive tribesmen lie in ambush behind every rock and every wadi, the Afghanistans brood behind the tribesmen, and behind them both stand the Russians!"

The General laughed.

"That is good, Meredith. Very good! I must remember that!"

"But what does Russia want?" Mrs. Onslow enquired.

"That is simple to answer," Major Meredith replied. "The prize is India!"

"Do they really think they can conquer us?"

"They would certainly attempt to do so if they got the chance," he said. "Geographically there is a protective mountain barrier round the North and West face of India — the Karakorums, the Pamirs, and the Hindu Kush."

"Well then?" Mrs. Onslow questioned.

"Russia is greedy. We have no desire to advance from India against Russia because that would be beyond the range of our sea power, but Russia, as you well know, can make things very difficult for us and has already done so for the last ten years by stirring up trouble in Afghanistan."

"I did hear," Colonel Onslow said, "that General Komaroff has sixty thousand men only a day's march from Herat. If that is true, though it may be a rumour, we should have to fight."

"We are always fighting to prevent Russian infiltration, Russian aggression, Russian influence on the tribesmen," Major Meredith said quietly, "and I do not think that things are more explosive at this moment than they have been in the past few years. Nevertheless we shall learn more when we reach Bombay."

Orissa had listened fascinated by the conversation. Now she felt that she must have out-stayed her welcome and as Major Meredith turned to say something to Colonel Onslow, she bent forward to murmur in Lady Critchley's ear:

"I think I should go and see if Neil is all right."

"Yes, of course, Mrs. Lane. Good-night," Lady Critchley said.

Orissa rose quickly and moved away from the table before anyone realised that she was about to do so and there was no need for the gentlemen to rise to their feet.

She walked across the Saloon conscious as she did so that the other passengers having their coffee looked at her as she passed.

She managed to appear indifferent to their attention, but when she reached the door she hurried as quickly as she could to her cabin.

She entered, shut the door behind her and then stood with her back to it as if it were a protection against what was outside.

'How could it be possible,' she asked herself, 'that Major Meredith should be on board this particular ship?'

It must, she thought, have been a chance in a million that they would ever encounter each other again, yet her heart was still beating violently in her breast from the shock of seeing him so unexpectedly.

She thought now she should have looked at the Passenger List when she first came on board. It was, she knew, always pinned up outside the Purser's office. Yet even if she had seen the name, what could she have done about it?

It would have been impossible to go ashore and equally impossible to remain in her cabin for the whole voyage.

But as it happened, everything was all right.

He had not recognised her — she was sure of it!

There had not been even a flicker of recognition or interest in his eyes and she felt if there had been she would not, agitated though she was, have missed it.

But she would have to be careful — very careful. Charles had said Major Meredith was "snoopy". But there was not the slightest reason in the world why he should make enquiries about her. And if he did — who could tell him anything?

General and Lady Critchley had believed the story told them by the Adjutant, and there was no-one else who was likely ever to have seen her before or have any idea she was not who she pretended to be.

'I am safe . . . quite safe!' Orissa told herself reassuringly as she started to undress.

Yet she found it was impossible to dismiss Major Meredith from her mind. There was something disturbing about him; something even in the tone of his voice that affected her.

When she got into her bunk she went over in her mind all the things Charles had told her about him.

He was thought to have been responsible for Gerald Dewar's death. That in itself was enough to condemn him, apart from the fact that he had had Charles "on the mat", as her brother would have described it, which was certainly something Orissa resented.

'He will spoil the voyage for me,' she told herself. Then with her natural resilience she determined she would not allow him to do so.

She had escaped by a miracle. By some marvellous chance of Fate she had been spirited away from the misery, humiliation and degradation she had suffered these past years at the hands of her Step-mother.

From being, as it seemed to her, confined in a dark cupboard, the doors were suddenly opened to light and hope.

She was going back to India! She was returning to the land she loved and which had always meant home.

Already she imagined she could feel the sun and see the beauty which had remained in her mind all through her unhappiness in

England like an oasis of wonder and joy.

She shut her eyes and thought as she had thought so often before, of the heat, the colour of the fruit and vegetables and grain in the Bazaar, the smell of musk, spices and ghee, mustard oil and masala.

She could remember the silk shops with their gay bales piled high, the jostling, drifting crowds, the great lazy sacred Brahmini bulls, sacred to Shiva.

And over it all the brilliant, burning sunshine, golden and blinding, enveloping her like the love for which she had been starved all these years in the cold and rain of London.

'Forget Major Meredith,' Orissa told herself. 'It is India that matters!'

Chapter Three

The next day they ran into bad weather.

When Orissa awoke she heard the straining shrouds and guy ropes creaking in the force of a high wind and the splash of the spray as it drove over the bows.

The ship was rolling and pitching and Neil began to feel sick from the moment he awoke.

He was tearful and irritable between bouts of vomiting and Orissa, aware at first of a queasy feeling, soon found she had no time to think of herself.

The Steward brought dismal accounts of the other passengers.

"All incapacitated, Ma'am," he told Orissa. "It's always the same this time of the year. The Dining-Saloon is deserted!"

It was impossible for Orissa to leave Neil, so the steward brought their luncheon to the cabin, and she coaxed the child to eat something knowing it was better to be sick on a full stomach rather than an empty one.

She tried to amuse him by telling him a story but after a while he fell asleep and she decided it would be a good opportunity to have a little fresh air.

By now it seemed as if she had found her "sea-legs" and she no longer felt sick, but she had a painful headache from the stuffiness of the cabin.

She put on her cloak and bonnet and, after asking the Steward to look in every ten minutes or so to see if Neil had awakened, she started an unsteady passage to the more sheltered side of the ship.

It was not easy to walk and she had to hold on to whatever she could on the way.

However she had a longing for fresh air and finally she let herself out onto the deserted deck which was heaving up and down beneath her feet.

It was impossible to walk about. The sea was so rough and the wind so strong that she knew that if she went near the rail her cloak might be whipped away from her, and certainly her bonnet would go at the first gust.

She could only therefore stand supported against the outside wall of the cabins sheltered from the rush and spray of the waves but still encountering some of the more violent blows of the wind which beat the tendrils of her hair against her cheeks so furiously that they hurt.

Yet she felt there was an exhilaration in it.

It seemed part of her own mood of getting free — of trying against impossible odds to escape from everything she hated in England.

The noise of the storm prevented her from hearing a door open and the first intimation that she was not alone came when a deep voice beside her said:

"I see you are a good sailor, Mrs. Lane."

She turned her head to see Major Meredith standing there, his grey eyes on her face and she was instantly conscious that she must look untidy.

"I am proud to find that I am," she answered. "I was not certain when I awoke if I would succumb like the poor little boy I am looking after."

"He is all right?" Major Meredith enquired.

"He is asleep," Orissa replied.

She had the strange feeling they were making desultory conversation which was of no importance, when they should be speaking of other things.

Then she remembered how dangerous Major Meredith could be and how Charles was afraid of him.

She decided that because of this she must be as ordinarily polite and pleasant as any woman in her position would be if a man of Major Meredith's social consequence condescended to her.

A sudden lurch of the ship made her stagger for a moment and Major Meredith's hand went out as if he would support her, but he did not in actual fact touch her.

Orissa looked away from him towards the green waves at one moment curving high and next swinging low in a swirl of white-crested water.

"You look as if you are enjoying it," he said.

She thought there was a mocking note in his voice.

"I am," she answered simply. "There is something exhilarating and exciting in the ship pitting its strength against all the might of the ocean."

"You are not afraid?"

"I think I should only be afraid if we had to turn back," Orissa replied.

"That is unlikely," Major Meredith remarked. "But it surprises me that you are so glad to leave England."

"Why?"

He seemed to consider a moment before

76

he answered:

"Most women find life in India constricting and narrow. The majority long passionately for home."

The word "home" brought Orissa sharp memories.

"To me India is home," she said.

She had the feeling that Major Meredith was going to question her further, and because she realised this must not happen she turned.

"I must go back to my charge, he may be needing me."

She had hardly completed the sentence before a violent roll of the ship made her lose her balance.

For one frightening moment it seemed as if she would slither down the sloping deck and be thrown against the railing over which the water was flooding.

She gave a little cry of fright, and at that moment a strong hand caught her wrist and pulled her back sharply so that she found herself in Major Meredith's arms.

It all happened so quickly. The impact of his hard body against the softness of hers made it difficult to breathe and she found his face very close to hers.

She was looking into his grey eyes.

Just for a moment time seemed suspended. Then with a little inarticulate murmur of apology, Orissa found it possible to reach the door.

Without looking back she hurried to her cabin.

Only when she was safely inside the Stateroom to find Neil still asleep did she sit down, feeling as if she had been buffetted not only by the wind, but in some inexplicable way by Major Meredith.

She had gone to sleep thinking of him, afraid for Charles and yet at the same time convinced that he had not recognised her. There had not been the smallest flicker of recognition in his eyes.

Again this morning she was certain that he did not connect her with the woman he had seen creeping up and again down the dark stairs of the house in Queen Anne Street — otherwise surely he would have betrayed his knowledge in one way or another.

Nevertheless, because of the things Charles had told her about Major Meredith, because for her own sake he was a very undesirable acquaintance, she felt she must do her best to avoid him.

It was not difficult during the next four days when the weather in the Bay of Biscay was extremely rough, and even Orissa felt it was unwise to venture onto the wave-swept decks.

She suffered from being confined in the cabin with Neil, but it gave her a chance to get on with making her new dresses in the pretty muslins she had bought in London. She also re-furbished her green gown with the tulle and ribbons.

She found that Neil was quite happy to lie and do nothing if she told him a story, and it was easy to sew at the same time.

Her dresses progressed apace, and it was when they were nearing Gibraltar that Orissa thought of a different way to occupy what free time she might have.

She had noticed the first night that there were a number of Indian passengers in the First Class Dining-Saloon.

She longed to make their acquaintance, to talk to them, and, most of all to find out if her knowledge of their language was still as good as it had been when she was a child.

At that time, because her Ayah talked to her in her own tongue, Orissa had found it as easy to converse with the natives as to talk English to her own family.

She was however well aware that Lady Critchley would think it very strange if she were to become friendly with the Indians on board, and she therefore thought of a better plan.

She went in search of the Purser, a red-faced, jolly man who was excellent at performing the most important part of his duties, which was to keep the passengers happy.

"I wonder if it would be possible," Orissa said, "for you to find anyone on board who would give me a few lessons in Urdu."

"Do you mean an Indian, Mrs. Lane?" the Purser enquired.

"Perhaps there is one on the Second or Third Class deck who would be grateful for a little extra money," she replied. "I could not pay much."

"I understand that," the Purser said. "I will see if there is anyone suitable but if they are not travelling First Class, I shall have to ask the Captain's permission for them to be allowed on this deck."

"The lessons would have to be after I have put my charge to bed," Orissa said, "and that would mean that they would really have to be after dinner. I usually retire once the coffee has been served."

"I have noticed that," the Purser said. "You are not a card-player, Mrs. Lane?"

"I cannot afford to gamble," Orissa said with a smile.

"Well I will certainly see what I can do to

help you," the Purser promised, "and I am sure that as several people are getting off at Malta it will be easy to find you a cabin that you can use."

"Thank you very much indeed," Orissa said.

She felt excited at the idea of "rubbing up" the language which she knew must have grown rusty over the years. Yet it seemed that every word she had ever spoken was still vividly in her mind.

Sometimes when she was walking to school, or sitting alone in the dismal house at Eaton Place, she would deliberately name English objects aloud in Urdu, liking the sound of them on her tongue.

By the time they reached Gibraltar the Dining-Saloon was full again and Neil went down to luncheon with his grandparents.

Despite Orissa's resolution to avoid Major Meredith as much as possible, she could not help being aware that when he was present at meal times the whole conversation seemed charged with interest.

At Malta it was Major Meredith who brought the news that there had been a victory for the Nile Expedition at Abu Klea Wells.

"A victory?" the General asked sharply.

Everyone at the table paused to listen,

81

their eyes riveted on Major Meredith's face.

"General Stewart has reported that he has fought a successful battle twenty-five miles from the river."

"Was it a big one?" the General enquired.

"Apparently he had ten thousand natives against him," Major Meredith answered, "but reports of what happened are not very detailed at the moment."

Orissa thought of a battle involving ten thousand of the enemy and found herself shivering. Very soon Charles would be fighting and she could not bear the thought of it.

"What news of General Gordon?" the General enquired.

"Apparently a message from the General dated December 29th stated: 'Khartoum all right — could hold out for years!' "

"How did they get that?" Colonel Onslow enquired.

"From what I gather it was written on a diminutive piece of paper that a native could secret about his person," Major Meredith answered. "The report says the man was actually stripped by some hostile Arabs, searched and beaten, but he managed to get his tiny message to Korte."

"Is there no news since December 29th?" Colonel McDougal enquired.

"If there is, they do not know of it in Malta," Major Meredith replied.

The other news they learnt from the foreign newspapers that came aboard was that there had been a dynamite attack in the House of Commons and the Tower of London.

"Good gracious!" Lady Critchley exclaimed, "I cannot imagine what the world is coming to! Who could have done such a thing?"

"They call themselves the 'Irish Invincibles' but they come from America," Major Meredith informed her. "The Chamber in the House of Commons was practically wrecked and special damage was done to the Government Front Bench."

"I can hardy credit such things happening in England!" Mrs. Onslow exclaimed. "One can hardly bear to think of the world and the mess it is in at the moment!"

"That is true," Lady Critchley agreed.

"Although I must say," Mrs. Onslow went on, "we ourselves should be thankful that we escaped from being ship-wrecked in that terrible storm."

"I do not think we were ever in danger of foundering," Colonel McDougal reassured her. "I saw in the newspapers a week ago that there were in fact four hundred and eleven fewer ship-wrecks last year than in 1883 and twelve hundred fewer lives were lost."

"I also read that report," Major Meredith remarked dryly, "and although the figures were encouraging, there were still three thousand people who perished at sea during the year!"

"Oh, do let us talk of something more cheerful," Mrs. Onslow begged. "I am sick of wars and explosions, and of hearing of people being drowned."

Unexpectedly she smiled across the table at Orissa.

"I am sure, Mrs. Lane, that like me, you have been longing to see the newspapers so that you could read of the engagement of Princess Beatrice to Prince Henry Battenburg? That is far more interesting to us women, do you not agree?"

"Yes, of course," Orissa answered politely.

She could not say that she found it impossible not to listen intently to everything Major Meredith said.

It was not only that she wanted to hear the news he had to impart, and she realised that he was in a privileged position so that he had access to military information wherever they docked, but there was something in his deep voice she found irresistible.

After a number of meals in his presence she found herself watching for him coming across the Dining-Saloon and wondering why he seemed to be outstanding even though there was nothing particularly arresting about his appearance.

He was of medium height, his hair a nondescript dark brown, his features were clear-cut but not particularly distinguished.

His face was thin and his cheek-bones stood out because of it.

In a photograph, she decided, he would look quite an ordinary English gentleman, and yet in real-life there was something about him which was different from other men.

Perhaps it was his eyes, a cynical twist of his lips, perhaps an authority or sense of purpose which it was difficult to describe.

She wondered what he did with most of the day on board because he was never in the Saloon before meals and usually joined the table after everyone else was seated.

She learned too that he never played any of the card-games which the other passengers found the only way to enliven the boredom of the voyage.

They also grumbled disagreeably on Sundays when there was no Whist or bezique and even smoking was frowned upon.

There was sunshine in the Mediterranean but the evenings were still chill until they drew nearer to Alexandria. Orissa then insisted on Neil walking round and round the deck for exercise and she also discovered other ways of keeping him in the fresh air.

She found among his belongings a painting box and a book which had a few rather stereotyped pictures he could colour and also a number of blank pages.

She suggested to the little boy that he should paint a special picture every day which he could give to his mother when they reached Bombay.

He was delighted at the idea and Orissa found herself drawing animals and people which illustrated the stories she told him.

She had never been particularly good at sketching, unlike many of her contemporaries who were prepared to spend hours painting water colours of flowers, follies and Castles.

She could draw the outline of an elephant, sketch a recognisable tiger or song-bird but anything else was beyond her powers.

They were only a day away from Alexandria when their course converged with a battle-ship heading in the same direction as themselves.

Excitedly Neil ran back to the cabin to fetch his drawing-book.

"Ship for Mama," he cried excitedly handing it to Orissa who looked rather helplessly at the big ship with its centre funnel and two tall masts.

She sat down on a deck-chair and balanced the book on her knee.

"Draw all the flags," Neil commanded as the battle-ship's pennants swung out in the wind and Orissa thought that they must be signalling to the *Dorunda*.

"It is not going to be easy to draw that big ship," Orissa remarked.

"But I thought you were so talented, Mrs. Lane," a voice said mockingly and she had no need to look round to know who spoke.

"She's drawing a big ship for me," Neil explained conversationally.

He was not a shy child having always been brought up with a number of adults around him.

"That is HMS *Agamemnon,*" Major Meredith said, "and for your information, Mrs. Lane, it is Britain's very latest double-screw, armour-plated turret ship."

"That makes it a lot easier to draw!" Orissa replied sarcastically.

"And do not forget to put in the four

heavy guns," Major Meredith admonished.

"If it is so easy, you had better do it yourself," Orissa said handing him the drawing-book and pencil.

She had expected him to refuse but instead he took the book from her and sitting down in the chair began to sketch the ship so that it covered the whole page.

To her surprise she found he could draw very well.

"Where is the ship going?" Neil enquired.

"To join the British Naval Squadron on the China Station," Major Meredith answered.

The ship was becoming easily recognisable under his skilful pencil.

"You are really an artist!" Orissa exclaimed.

"You flatter me!" he replied.

"Sketching was never one of my hobbies," she said, watching with fascinated eyes the ship come to life on the paper.

"And what are they?" Major Meredith asked.

"History and Literature," Orissa answered truthfully.

"I felt you would like history," Major Meredith remarked.

"Why should you think that?" Orissa enquired. Then wondered if the conversation was too personal.

Major Meredith did not answer her question. Instead he finished his drawing, handed it to her and said:

"You should explain to Neil that the *Agamemnon* replaces the old wooden line-of-battle-ship of the same name which was in the bombardment of the forts of Sebastapol."

"Does it really?" Orissa's eyes were alight with interest. "I have always been interested in the Battle of Sebastapol."

"We were as usual up against the Russians," Major Meredith said.

"Are things serious in India?"

Despite her resolution not to show too great an interest in Army matters, Orissa could not help the question.

"Very serious," Major Meredith answered, "but most people are not aware of it."

As if he wished to say no more, he walked away from her to the railing where Neil was standing staring at the battleship.

He stayed for a short while talking to the small boy, telling him about the ship, explaining the meaning of the pennants. Then without speaking again to Orissa he walked away.

Neil spent the afternoon colouring the

drawing that Major Meredith had drawn so skilfully.

The following morning they reached Alexandria and there was plenty to see and to draw in the busy Port.

To Orissa's disappointment, Lady Critchley decided it would be unwise for Neil to go ashore in case he picked up some disease. So Orissa, knowing that almost everyone else on the ship was taking the opportunity of exploring the town, had to stay behind.

At the same time, she forced herself not to complain or feel ill-used.

She was so fortunate to be on the voyage at all, and if she was obliged to put up with some disappointments it was a small price to pay for escaping from her Step-mother.

When they reached Port Said, again she had to accept the disappointment of not going ashore but everybody was back on board before dinner as the ship was to start its slow journey down the Suez Canal at 9 o'clock.

They were all seated as usual in the Dining-Saloon before Major Meredith appeared, and when he did, Orissa thought even before he reached the table that something had occurred.

She could not tell how she knew it, she was only sure that there was something in his bearing, or perhaps in his expression, that was different.

He took his seat before he said to the General in a low voice, which was nevertheless perfectly audible to everyone else at the table:

"I thought you would wish to know, Sir, that Khartoum has fallen!"

"I cannot believe it!" the General exclaimed. "And General Gordon?"

"Reports, not yet confirmed are that he has been killed!"

The General banged his fist down heavily on the table.

"If any one man is responsible for this," he said angrily, "it is the Prime Minister. It was unbelievable that he should have delayed so long in sending out an Expeditionary Force."

"I have always said that at seventy-seven Mr. Gladstone is too old to hold such an office," Lady Critchley said tartly.

"Poor General Gordon!" Mrs. Onslow cried. "He was so brave and so confident that Khartoum would not fall."

"The British troops should have reached it in time!" Colonel McDougal exclaimed. "The whole thing must have been disgracefully mishandled."

"I think we must wait," Major Meredith

said quietly, "before passing judgment. There is no doubt that the troops encountered unexpected difficulties when they reached the Cataracts."

"What will happen now?" the General asked.

"I have no idea, Sir."

"You think Sir Charles and Major Kitchener will withdraw?"

"It is difficult to hazard a guess at this distance," Major Meredith replied. "It depends on whether they think they have enough troops to meet and defeat the Mahdi's army."

"Rabble! Natives armed with spears!" the General murmured contemptuously.

"The Mahdi is a brilliant leader of men," Major Meredith replied, "and you must remember, Sir, that it is a religious war. Men fight fanatically when they are inspired by Faith."

That was true, Orissa thought, and wondered whether the General or the two Colonels at the table would understand as apparently Major Meredith did, that a man's belief in his cause gave him a greater strength.

General Gordon's death caused a gloom on the party and Orissa was glad to escape when dinner was over.

The Purser had not failed her and had found in the Third Class an Indian called Mr. Mahla who had been a teacher in England at one of the London Universities.

He was a man of about thirty-five who was returning to India with his family.

He was very dark-skinned, coming from Bengal. His thick black shining hair was brushed back from a square forehead. His features were fine-cut.

But he looked desperately tired, older than his age and his elegant dark blue eyes often held an expression of despair.

He was, Orissa discovered, extremely hard-up but, when she pressed him to accept a little more for the lessons than he had first asked, he told her proudly that he made arrangements with the Purser and would not even consider any increase.

It was a joy to be able to converse in fluent, liquid Urdu, and Orissa soon found that she had in fact not forgotten the language of her childhood.

All she really had to do was to enlarge her vocabulary since having been interested only in childish subjects when she had lived in India, she now had so many others on which she wished to converse.

It was fascinating to be able to discuss the developments which had taken place in

India during the last few years and even more interesting to talk of religion.

It was this subject Mr. Mahla had taught in England and whilst Orissa had a certain understanding of Buddhism, Hinduism and the Moslem faith, she had learnt a great deal from him in the few lessons he had already given her.

Every Indian wants to talk and, as they had set no particular time limit on how long her lessons should last, Orissa was not surprised, when finally Mr. Mahla rose almost reluctantly to his feet to say good-night, to find it was after midnight.

He bowed and made *Namaskar,* the traditional Indian salutation, fingers to fingers, palm to palm and the hands raised to the level of his forehead.

Orissa walked to her cabin to find Neil was fast asleep.

On an impulse she decided to go out on deck, and picked up the glittering scarf she wore over all her evening gowns.

She could hear as she moved across the ship the sound of laughter and raised voices from the Smoking-Saloon, where there was a Bar, and she had a glimpse of a number of passengers in the Card-room speaking only in low voices as they concentrated on their game.

The big Saloon was almost empty and she was sure that the General and Lady Critchley had long since retired to bed.

She went out on deck and moving for'ard stood against the rail to look out into the night.

The ship was passing very slowly through the Canal, the little pilot-ship with its red and green lights puffing ahead of them. They moved so slowly it was almost as if they stood still and even the engines were quiet.

Far away, as far as the eye could see, there was the vast emptiness of the desert sands, but above the sky was brilliant with stars and a crescent moon was adding its light to the heavens.

It was so lovely that Orissa could only draw in her breath. It seemed to be part of all she had been talking about with Mr. Mahla. She felt it almost explained without words the subjugation of Self, the instinct for perfection.

"What does it look like to you?" a voice beside her asked.

Somehow she was not surprised to find that Major Meredith had joined her.

"I was trying to put that into words for myself," she answered.

It was as if they had been talking for a

long time and their discussion had not just begun but had been continuous.

He did not speak and she went on:

"It is so beautiful, so unbelievably, wonderfully beautiful! And yet at the same time it is frightening!"

"Why?"

"Because it makes me realise how small and unimportant I am. Every one of those stars may hold millions of other people like us looking, wondering and trying to understand."

"What do they want to understand?"

"That is the question that mankind has asked since the beginning of time . . . why he was not given the power to understand himself."

"And you find yourself an enigma?"

"But of course," Orissa answered. "Ever since I was a child I have asked 'Who am I?' and hoped that I would one day know the answer."

"It should not be very difficult for someone like you."

His voice seemed to deepen on the last word.

"But it is!" Orissa answered. "More difficult than you can realize."

"Why could I not realize what you are trying to say?"

"Because . . . I cannot explain it . . . I only know that when I look at the world like this I feel . . . so very small, helpless and alone."

Orissa raised her head to look up at the stars as she spoke.

The man watching could see the perfection of her profile — the soft sensitiveness of her lips and the lovely line of her neck very white in the starlight against the faint glitter of the spangled scarf she wore around her shoulders.

It was a movement of grace, so beautiful and some ways so spiritual that for a moment he drew in his breath.

Then in a voice which held an undeniable hint of mockery in it he said:

"If that is what is troubling you there is no need for loneliness."

As he spoke he put his arms around her and drew her almost roughly against him.

As her head fell back against his shoulder — his lips were on hers!

For a moment Orissa was numb with surprise, so that she could not think; could not take in what had happened!

Then when she should have thrust him away, it was impossible to move.

The hard insistence of his lips held her captive. She felt as if his arms imprisoned her and yet at the same time gave her a sense of security and belonging.

She had never been kissed before and the strange mystical feeling that seemed to possess her was something that was not a human emotion but a narcotic which drugged her mind until she could not think.

It was strange and yet at the same time so utterly and completely wonderful that the stars, the darkness of the night, and the moon were a part of the man who possessed her.

His lips were a warm, demanding wonder, which left her a hollow shell of herself and she felt as if she passed into his keeping.

Then at last he raised his lips from hers the spell was broken and she was free.

With a little gasp of horror she pushed her hands against his chest and incapable of speech, knowing only that she was frightened to the point of panic, she turned and ran away from him.

He stood where she had left him, seeing the frilled tulle of her bustle following her like a small, crested wave; the shimmering scarf glinting in the light of the stars.

Then there was only darkness and he could see her no longer.

When she reached her cabin Orissa shut the door quietly and flung herself down on the bunk to hide her face against the pillow.

It could not have happened . . . it could not be true! How could he have behaved in such a manner . . . or she permit it?

She knew the answer as clearly as if he told her so.

He had recognised her! He had known! He had seen her in Queen Anne Street and he had thought what she had expected he would think when he was aware she had spent the night in Charles's rooms!

It was obvious, Orissa thought with burning cheeks, that no gentleman would behave in such a manner to a girl he thought was pure and respectable.

But to treat in this way a married woman, who had a husband in India and a lover in London, was behaviour to which she was unlikely to take exception.

She had to admit, she had invited it upon herself. In speaking of being lonely, she was talking of the soul, but he had thought she spoke of her body.

Going back over their conversation she could understand that Major Meredith, believing her to be a loose woman, unfaithful to her husband, would find it incomprehensible that she should not welcome his advances or enjoy a flirtation, if not more, when the opportunity arose.

'I am ashamed! I am ashamed!' Orissa whispered into her pillow.

She knew she could blame no-one for what had happened except perhaps her Step-mother for having forced her to take refuge with her brother.

Yet how could she have anticipated that out of all the ships sailing to India, Major Meredith would have been on the *Dorunda* or that because she was in the company of the Critchleys it was impossible for her to avoid him.

She might have guessed those searching grey eyes would not have been deceived.

Thinking over again and again what had occurred on the landing at Charles's lodgings, she had hoped that because the gaslight was behind her her face would have been unrecognisable.

Nor did she think that he would have remembered her figure; the way she moved, the darkness of her hair.

'I have been living in a Fool's Paradise,' Orissa told herself and knew there was nothing she could do, no explanation she could make to him.

What she had to try and find was an explanation to herself as to why Major Meredith's lips had held her captive so that she had made no effort to escape until he allowed her to do so.

How could she have been so helpless, so acquiescent?

How indeed could she have surrendered her pride and her sense of decency so that she had in fact behaved like the woman she pretended to be rather than a young girl who had never previously been touched by man.

She could not explain her behaviour to herself.

Yet it had happened and she could not deny it had been part of the glory of the night and something unexpectedly wonderful that no words could take away.

She had the feeling that if he had gone on kissing her she would still be in his arms.

She could not deny to herself that to be so close to him had given her a sense of security; a feeling of being safe that she had not known since she was a child.

'It was all just part of my . . . imagination,' Orissa said sternly and yet she knew that was untrue.

But what concerned her now was that tomorrow she would have to see him again, to sit at the same table; and know what he was thinking of her.

She would feel even if she was not looking at him that his eyes were looking into her

101

soul and believing it to be smirched and dirty.

"I cannot bear it! I cannot meet him!" she whispered aloud and yet there was nothing she could do.

She was caught! The ship was a cage from which there was no escape.

Wildly in her imagination Orissa thought of diving over-board and swimming ashore to disappear into the desert, but that was only a fantasy.

Tomorrow would bring reality. She must meet him again, know that she had been compliant to his will and apparently not outraged by the manner in which he had treated her.

"I must have been mad!" she told herself, but she knew that if it had been madness it was very sweet.

Never had she realised that she could know anything so magical and entrancing.

Never had she imagined that her whole being would throb because a man touched her lips. Or that all the poetry and all the beauty of the world could be contained in a feeling that had run through her body when it seemed no longer to be her own but to belong to him.

"It cannot have happened!" Orissa cried despairingly.

But it had!

And there was nothing she could do about it!

CHAPTER FOUR

Orissa approached Lady Critchley early the next morning.

"I think," she said, "that Neil would eat a better meal if I gave it to him alone. It is clear that he becomes distracted by people talking and I am very anxious he should put on weight before he arrives in India."

"Perhaps that is a good idea, Mrs. Lane," Lady Critchley agreed.

Having managed to avoid seeing Major Meredith at luncheon Orissa had no compunction about saying she would dine in her own cabin and not come down to dinner.

There were only seven days left at sea before they reached Bombay. During the night when she had remained awake going over what had happened, she decided that if she were clever, it should be possible, even though they were confined in the ship, to avoid meeting Major Meredith.

She had the idea, although she was not certain, that he took his exercise early in the day before the majority of the passengers were up.

She did not know why he spent so much time in his cabin. She guessed it had something to do with reports, perhaps making adverse comments on Charles's behaviour when he was in London!

When she thought of it she tried to hate him but found it impossible!

She had only to remember the way he kissed her to feel again that strange warmth steal over her body and know the sudden rapture which had made her his prisoner.

Yet she was determined not to think of it, or of him, if she could possibly help it.

She forced herself to pay more attention to little Neil; to play games with him when they went on deck when the other passengers were about and she was quite certain there would be no sign of Major Meredith.

Neil enjoyed deck-quoits and she tried to teach him Badminton. She borrowed a pack of cards from the card-room and built him card-castles in the cabin.

The book which he was painting for his mother was nearly filled, with strange animals and people who had only sticks for arms and circles for faces.

They in no way compared with the expertise of the ship which Major Meredith had sketched.

Orissa also finished sewing her dresses and altered the others she had brought with her so that they looked more fashionable.

They acquired a grace and elegance when she wore them which was however more due to the fact that she had a perfect figure than to anything else.

Fortunately there were quite a number of books in the ship's library which she wished to read; but even so, she would find herself staring at a page for a long time and realising she had not read a word.

It was very hot in the Red Sea. One evening it became so stifling in the cabin that even Mr. Mahla complained of it.

"Why should we not have our lessons on deck?" Orissa asked, realising that she too felt confined in the airless State-room.

It was getting late and she thought there would be few passengers on deck and when they reached it, it was in fact deserted. Orissa went to two deck-chairs far forward in the bow and they pulled them out to sit clear of the awning right against the railing which encircled the top deck.

There was just a faint breeze but not

enough to fill the sails and the ship was rely-
ing entirely on its engines.

Again the stars threw a mystical light over
the universe and the reflection of the lights
from the ship on the smooth sea was very
beautiful.

Orissa sat down and Mr. Mahla seated
himself beside her.

"Are you looking forward to being home
again?" she asked in his own language.

He shook his head.

"No?" she questioned.

"I wished to stay in England," Mr. Mahla
replied. "I enjoyed my position at the
University. It was very interesting and I had
many friends."

"Then why are you going back?"

"I have to go! My father has died and now
I am head of the family. There is my mother
to care for and I have four brothers, three
sisters and their children who are all de-
pending on me."

"You mean that you will have to give up
working as a teacher?" Orissa asked.

He nodded and she could see by the lights
of the stars that his eyes were dark and
miserable.

"We have a little land," he said. "I must
work on it for the good of the family."

"Then your literary achievements will be wasted."

"It is my Karma — my Fate."

"Do you really believe," Orissa asked, "that you have no choice in the matter?"

"None."

"But I cannot think that is true," she protested. "Is it all ordained what we shall do, what is to happen to us?"

"That is what I believe," Mr. Mahla answered.

"How can you be sure that you are not imagining such a thing?" Orissa asked, "and just accepting everything that occurs however bad, as inevitable without fighting against it?"

"It is all written in our hands," Mr. Mahla offered.

"I have heard that," Orissa said, "and yet I can hardly credit that it is true."

"Look at the lines on your palm," he suggested. "Every line is different. No two human beings have the same marks. There is the story of one's life. There are the lines of fate very clear for us to see."

"Can you read your own fate?" Orissa enquired. "Can you read other people's?"

"Sometimes," he answered.

She put out her left hand, palm upwards towards him.

"What do you see in mine?"

Very delicately Mr. Mahla supported her fingers with the first two of his right hand.

Looking down into her small palm he said:

"Can you not see your line of Fate running almost from your wrist to the base of your middle finger? It is a very straight line. It denotes not only strength of character and tenacity but also that your life is preordained. You are a very old soul, Mrs. Lane."

"Tell me more," Orissa begged fascinated.

Then as he raised her hand a trifle higher to catch the light from the Heavens above there was a shadow beside them.

Orissa looked up and felt her heart give a frightened leap.

It was Major Meredith who stood there and she knew although she was not certain whether she saw it in his eyes or merely sensed it, that he was in a towering rage.

"You do not belong to this deck!" he said sharply to Mr. Mahla.

For a moment both Orissa and the Indian teacher stiffened.

Then Mr. Mahla rose to his feet made his usual obeisance to Orissa and moved away before she could prevent him.

She was so surprised at Major Meredith's behaviour that for a moment she could not think, and the words would not come to her lips. Before she could speak he said:

"It would be wiser, Mrs. Lane, if you kept your favours to your own class and to your own colour!"

For a second Orissa did not understand what he was saying, and then as a blush burnt her cheeks, she lost her temper!

"How dare you speak to me like that!" she said in a voice that was low and vibrant with fury. "How dare you make such suggestions or infer such motives for my actions! Whatever I do it is none of your business, but I suppose that in your usual manner you are interfering in other people's affairs."

She drew in her breath before she went on:

"I have heard about you, Major Meredith. I know how you involve yourself in matters which do not concern you, and how you snoop around trying to make trouble."

She saw the surprise in his face at the manner in which she was speaking, but now she did not care.

"And having discovered something wrong," she continued in a scathing tone but all the more violent because she kept it low, "you harrass the person, making their lives a misery until, like poor Gerald Dewar, they shoot themselves!"

"What are you saying? How do you know this?" Major Meredith asked and there was no disguising the astonishment in his tone.

"I know that I despise and hate you!" Orissa cried. "I have tried to keep out of your way after the manner in which you insulted me the other night, but it seems you are determined to interfere in my private life. Leave me alone, Major Meredith! All I ask is that you leave me alone!"

She turned as she spoke and walked away, not running frantically as she had done the last time they had been on deck together, but with her head held high.

She was however shaking with shock and anger and only when she had passed through the door which led into the accommodation did she run to the sanctuary of her own cabin.

She shut the door and with her cheeks burning and her breath coming jerkily from sheer rage, she walked across the cabin to stand staring at herself in the mirror on the dressing-table.

She could see the whiteness of her neck and arms against the red of her evening gown.

It was the same dress she had worn, she

remembered, the first time she had seen Major Meredith when she had been creeping up the stairs to Charles's room.

Perhaps it was unlucky. Perhaps there was something about the colour of it which attracted trouble.

Then she told herself the only thing that was really unlucky was that she had come in contact with Major Meredith.

How dare he think such things of her? How dare he?

At the same time some logical part of her mind told her that it was not to be expected that he should think anything else.

Always he seemed to find her in incriminating circumstances: the memory of her coming down the stairs of a gentleman's lodging at 6 o'clock in the morning would obviously be enough to make him sure that Mr. Mahla had been holding her hand romantically in the star-light!

As she thought about it she realised that as he had walked up the deck towards them they would have been silhouetted against the sky and there was no denying that the Indian had in fact been touching her fingers.

'But how can he think such things of me?' Orissa asked her reflection, and told herself in all honesty there was nothing else he could think.

'It does not matter! It is of no consequence! In a few days time I shall never have
to see him again,' she told herself.

Then she remembered Mr. Mahla's words
. . . that it was Karma . . . fate, and there
was no escaping it!

'That is nonsense!' Orissa tried to convince herself in a practical manner. 'We all
have free-will and we all make our lives the
way we want them.'

Yet her studies of Buddhism and a picture
of the Wheel of Re-birth came flooding into
her mind to question such an assertion.

Millions and millions of Orientals believed
in their fate and that there was nothing they
could do about it.

Could they all be wrong? Could the white
races with their self-assurance, their conceit
that they themselves were omnipotent, be
the only ones who were right?

In the meantime there was Mr. Mahla to
consider. What would he think of being
dismissed in such an arbitrary manner.

She had the feeling he would be sensible
enough to understand that Major
Meredith's anger was directed not against
him but against her.

It was impossible for the Indian not to
think there was something strange between
them when Major Meredith showed his

authority so obviously, and she had been too shocked and tongue-tied to do or say anything while he was still there.

Unhappy, still angry and yet at the same time deeply depressed at what had just taken place, Orissa undressed and got into her bunk to lie with sleepless eyes staring in the darkness.

She was half-afraid the following evening that Mr. Mahla would not come for their lesson.

It was in fact the one thing she looked forward to every day.

There was something soothing in talking in the lovely, eloquent language with its flowery, extravagant phrases; its soft vowels and words which were sheer poetry.

Even to speak in Urdu made Orissa feel that she had almost reached the end of her journey; that soon she would be home and know once again the warmth and love that she had missed so much these past years.

It was hard for her to realise she was not going to find her mother waiting for her, nor was she going to the Province of Orissa, where she had been born.

She had been to Delhi only once or twice in her life and she could hardly remember the ancient Mogul City. She had the feeling that it might now be very social.

For most of her years in India their home had been further North in the Punjab at Lahore — or at the city of roses Kapurtala with its pink villas and the peaks of the Himalayas.

But it did not really matter where she went, Orissa thought, so long as she was again in the country where she belonged.

She need not have worried about Mr. Mahla.

He arrived punctually at nine o'clock, greeted her quietly and with his usual exquisite courtesy as if nothing untoward had occurred the night before.

"I am so pleased to see you," Orissa said. "How is your family? They are well, I hope?"

She asked, as she always did, out of conventional politeness, but tonight Mr. Mahla instead of thanking her for her concern, replied:

"I am very worried."

"Worried?" Orissa asked. "Why?"

"My wife is not well. She had many pains all last night and today."

"Has she seen a doctor?"

Mr. Mahla shook his head.

"No. She will not do so. You understand, my wife does not understand English ways. She could not be examined by a man or even speak to one of her ailments."

"I understand, of course I understand," Orissa replied, knowing that such a thing would shock a Hindu woman and offend her modesty.

"I do not know what to do!" Mr. Mahla said. "My wife cries all the time. The pain is very bad."

"I expect she has eaten something that disagrees with her," Orissa replied. "Would you like me to visit her?"

"It is very kind of you to suggest it, but it is not possible for a lady in your position to come down to the Third Class Deck."

"But of course I can," Orissa answered. "Tell me again exactly what your wife is feeling."

Mr. Mahla explained to Orissa his wife's symptoms in some detail, and she was quite certain that the trouble was strange food combined with a touch of fever which was very prevalent in the heat of the Red Sea.

"I will tell you what I will do," Orissa said. "I will speak to the Ship's doctor and get some medicine from him which will at least alleviate your wife's pain. We will then go down and see her and afterwards we can come back here again to have our lesson."

"It is very kind, very gracious of you," Mr. Mahla exclaimed. "But I do not like to impose on your good nature."

"It is no imposition," Orissa smiled. "Just wait here while I go and find the doctor."

She found Dr. Thompson in his surgery.

Usually at this time he was in the Saloon, but apparently one of the passengers had cut his thumb on a broken glass and the doctor was bandaging it.

"I will not be a minute, Mrs. Lane," he said cheerfully when he saw Orissa.

She already knew Dr. Thompson because Lady Critchley had insisted on his examining Neil after the child had been so sea-sick passing through the Bay of Biscay.

Orissa had decided that he was neither a clever nor an ambitious man. But he was a good mixer and because he liked both comfort and the company of other people, he was quite content with his position as Ship's Doctor.

The patient with the bandaged thumb departed and Dr. Thompson said to Orissa,

"Now, Mrs. Lane, you look well enough! So I cannot believe you need my services."

"No, thank you, I do not," Orissa replied. "But there is a woman who does but who will not ask your help."

She explained to the doctor about Mrs. Mahla's illness and that she was the wife of her teacher.

She had the feeling that because the

117

Indian woman was a Third Class passenger, Dr. Thompson was quite glad not to have the bother of treating her.

"It is all the same with these Indians," he said in a disparaging tone. "They do not care for our type of food and practically starve themselves to death on the voyage. But the woman has not got long now before she will be back on rice and chapattes which suit her far better than anything else."

"In the meantime her husband says she is in considerable pain," Orissa said gently.

The doctor produced from a cupboard a bottle filled with a white-looking liquid.

"Tell him to give her two tablespoons of this every four hours," he said. "It should settle her stomach, and here are a few pills which will make her sleep."

"Thank you very much," Orissa said gratefully.

"It is more faith-healing than anything else with those people," the Doctor said. "Tell her to throw in a prayer to the right god and she'll soon be better."

Orissa thanked him again and carrying the medicine went back to the cabin where Mr. Mahla was waiting.

She told him what the Doctor had prescribed and he was profuse in his gratitude for her kindness in obtaining the medicines.

"Let us take them to your wife right away," Orissa suggested.

"You are quite certain you do not mind visiting my humble cabin?" Mr. Mahla asked. "My wife would deem it a very great honour that such a gracious lady should come to see her, but I do not wish to impose upon your good nature."

"It is no imposition," Orissa said. "I would very much like to meet your wife. I should have suggested it before."

They went down the stairways which led from the First Class Deck to the Second Class and again to the Third.

Despite the assurance Orissa had received from the Steward that the other decks were unusually comfortable she could not help noticing how hot and stifling it was below.

The passages were narrow, undecorated and the Mahlas' cabin when they reached it seemed far too small for the number of people it contained.

Mr. Mahla, Orissa learnt, had six children. The family was all packed, eight of them, into a cabin which was intended to hold four and there hardly seemed room to turn round.

There was no doubt that Mrs. Mahla was in pain.

She was lying down and groaning with her

hands crossed over her stomach but she made a great effort to try to sit up when her husband introduced Orissa.

"Do not move," Orissa begged. "I am here because I know you are ill and I have brought you some medicine which I hope will make you better."

"I am in pain — I shall die before we reach home," Mrs. Mahla groaned.

"I promise you will not do that," she said, "and you must think of the children. What will they do if you are too ill to look after them?"

The children, who ranged in age from a few months to a girl of perhaps ten years old seemed apparently to think this was their cue because they began to cry out to their mother that she must get well for their sakes.

They were all extremely pretty children. Orissa liked their large brown soulful eyes and the manner in which even the small ones managed to induce a soft pleading note into their musical voices.

She persuaded Mrs. Mahla to swallow tablespoonfuls of the Doctor's medicine right away. Then she gave her two pills which would make her sleep, and told the children they must be very quiet.

Because she realised that without his

wife's assistance Mr. Mahla seemed rather helpless, she helped him put the younger children into their bunks where two of them slept side by side.

She then fed the baby with some watery milk which was all that was obtainable on board, until the child closed its eyes and went to sleep.

Mr. Mahla put the baby in beside his wife who was so quiet and still that Orissa was certain that the sleeping-draught had taken effect.

"You have done so much for which I thank you," he said. "Now I will take you back."

"No, it is too late for our lesson," Orissa answered. "I will find my own way. You must stay and look after the children who must not wake their mother now she is asleep."

"You cannot find your way alone," he protested.

"Of course I can," Orissa answered. "I will not get lost, I promise you. Stay here, and I am sure when your wife has had a really good night, she will feel quite different in the morning."

"May you be blessed for your kindness," Mr. Mahla said and lifted his hands to his forehead.

Orissa smiled at him and slipped from the cabin.

It was very hot and outside she wiped her forehead with her handkerchief before she set out to retrace her steps along the narrow passages to the stair-way.

She had gone a little way when she heard laughter, noisy voices speaking in English and saw coming towards her three soldiers.

They were in uniform and she realised as they approached that they were all three drunk and unsteady on their feet.

There was no way she could avoid meeting them as the passage was so narrow.

She therefore walked on steadily towards them until as they appeared, with their arms round each other's shoulders, not inclined to make way for her, she stood against the side of the passage expecting them to pass.

But instead they came to a standstill.

"What've we 'ere?" one of them asked in a slurred voice. "Somethin' very pretty we ain't seen before."

"Someone we've certainly not seen before," another soldier remarked. "Where've yer been hiding yerself, dearie?"

He stuck his head forward to leer into Orissa's face and she felt a little tremor of fear as she managed to say quietly and with dignity:

"Kindly let me pass."

"Oh, us can't do that!" the third soldier

said jovially, "not 'til yer've told us awl about yerself!"

They stood closer to Orissa hemming her in. She could smell beer on their breath and the heat of their bodies seemed to be reaching out towards her making her feel uncertain and afraid.

"Will you please let me pass," she asked again.

Conscious that they towered over her she felt small, and insignificant, while her voice had not the tone of authority she would have wished.

"Wot's yer hurry?" asked the soldier who had spoken first. "Perhaps us'll let yer go if yer're kind t'us. We ain't seen a pretty gal like yer since we left Tilbury, 'ave we, boys?"

"That us ain't," the other man answered, "so yer must be a sport an' give us awl a kiss before us lets yer escape."

Orissa drew in her breath.

She wanted to scream for help. But she wondered whether in the depths of the ship anyone would hear her, and even if they did whether they would take any notice?

"Now come on then," one of the soldiers leered. "A kiss awl round an' us'll let yer go — if yer insists."

"That's if yer do insist," another laughed.

Orissa lifted her hands as if she would

fight her way through them and then as she opened her mouth to scream an authoritative voice asked:

"What is going on here?"

She thought she must cry out with relief.

The soldiers who had been bending towards her straightened themselves and made an unsteady effort to stand to attention.

"Return to your quarters immediately!" Major Meredith ordered.

The three men made an attempt at saluting him, then turned somewhat shamefacedly and shuffled down the passageway.

Orissa had one glance at Major Meredith's face and walked on the way she had been going. She knew that he was following her and was conscious that her heart was beating furiously.

At the same time she was overwhelmed with relief because he had come just at the right moment to save her.

She reached the staircase and he walked just one step behind her until they reached the broader stairway going from the Second Class to the Upper deck.

It was then that he moved to her side.

"What were you doing down there?" he questioned, "or need I ask?"

There was such a note of contempt in his

voice that Orissa drew in her breath.

So that was why he thought she had gone below!

He had imagined that the Indian with whom he suspected her of conducting a love-affair was too frightened to come to the First Class and so she had gone to him!

She felt her anger, hot and furious, rise within her, and then as it did so a sudden faintness swept over her.

It was partly the heat, partly the unpleasant experience of encountering the soldiers, and partly the fact that she had not slept the night before and had been able to eat nothing all day.

She had thought the food would choke her, but the absence of it left her curiously weak.

She felt now as if her head was very light and the darkness was coming up from the floor to cover her.

She reached out her hand towards the bannisters, made an inarticulate little sound and then even as she felt herself falling, Major Meredith caught her in his arms.

He lifted her as if she were a child, carried her up the remaining stairs, and pushing open the door of the Writing-room set her down in a leather arm-chair.

It was a small room which was seldom used.

Orissa put her head back and shut her eyes. She felt the whole ship was swimming round her and yet she was not completely unconscious.

She heard Major Meredith go to the door and give an order, and a few seconds later, although it may have been longer, she felt a glass against her lips.

"Drink this!"

She wanted to refuse, but there was something in his tone which made her obey him and she felt the fiery spirit leap like a flame down her throat.

It was almost agony, but when she would have pushed the glass away he commanded:

"A little more."

She wanted to argue but it was impossible to speak. It was easier to do what he wished. She drank some more of the brandy and no longer felt faint.

"I . . . am . . . sorry," she tried to say.

"Sit still!" Major Meredith commanded. "You will be all right in a moment."

She found it difficult to get her breath, and yet her brain was clearing. The faintness had gone and she felt the colour must have come back into her cheeks.

She was no longer desperately hot, on the

contrary now cold, and she felt Major Meredith take her hands in his, rubbing them gently to warm them.

"You will be all right in a moment," he said re-assuringly.

It was true. In another minute or two Orissa realised that she no longer felt weak and helpless but quite capable of returning to her own cabin.

She drew her hands away and opening her eyes said in what sounded almost a normal voice:

"Thank you very . . . much. I . . . regret having been such a . . . bother to . . . you."

"It is no bother," he said. "But surely you have enough sense . . ."

He stopped.

Perhaps because she still looked ill, perhaps because he felt that what he had to say was superfluous.

Orissa rose a little shakily to her feet. She walked across the Writing-room and Major Meredith opened the door for her.

They stepped out onto the wide landing at the top of the stairs up which he had carried her.

"Thank . . . you," Orissa said once again in a low voice without looking at him.

Then as she would have left the Doctor came from the Saloon.

"Hello, Mrs. Lane," he greeted her. "How did you get on with your Indian patient? Did you persuade her to take my medicines?"

Without turning her head Orissa was aware that Major Meredith had stiffened beside her.

"Mrs. Mahla took them both, Dr. Thompson," she said quietly, "and she was sleeping when I left her. I am sure she will be better in the morning."

"Let us hope so," the Doctor said jovially.

Then to Major Meredith he remarked:

"Good evening, Major. You see I have a very helpful assistant!"

Orissa did not stop to hear any more.

She walked to her cabin and as she shut the door she hoped that for the first time Major Meredith was discomfited.

The Doctor would tell him why she had gone down to the Third Class deck. He would learn that his suppositions, his insinuations were unfounded, and she hoped he would feel ashamed.

But nothing the Doctor would say could explain away the manner in which she had allowed Major Meredith to kiss her.

That was something which no-one could explain except herself and she could not find a solution.

She was still standing just inside her cabin when there came a knock at the door.

For a moment she thought that she had been mistaken. Then very quietly it came again.

She opened the door to find Major Meredith standing outside.

"I want to speak to you," he said.

"No!" she answered. "It is too . . . late. Besides . . ."

She glanced in the direction of the Stateroom next door which belonged to General and Lady Critchley.

"They are both in the Saloon," Major Meredith said, reading her thoughts, "but I must speak to you — you know that."

"There is nothing to say," Orissa answered.

"Yes there is," he contradicted. "You know I have to ask your forgiveness. I have only learnt this moment that the Indian is your teacher."

"I accept your apology for your . . . behaviour last night," Orissa said, "and now . . ."

She would have shut the door but Major Meredith held it open.

"You do not sound very forgiving," he said accusingly and there was laughter in his eyes.

"I am . . . tired and I wish to go to . . .

bed," she answered. "You cannot stay . . .
here talking to me as you . . . well know."

"Is it not rather late in the day for you
and me to worry about your reputation?"
he asked.

Orissa knew to what he was referring.

He might apologise for his misunderstand-
ing over Mrs. Mahla, but what he had
thought about her being in Charles's room
all night still lay between them like a naked
sword.

"Please leave me alone!" Orissa said. "We
have nothing more to say to each other!
Nothing!"

"Are you sure of that?"

"Quite sure!"

Her voice was positive and she knew that
he was somewhat nonplussed by her deter-
mination to be rid of him.

He would have said something else, but
there was the sound of voices in the distance
and he turned his head to see who was approaching.

Orissa seized her opportunity.

She shut the door and he could not help
hearing the key turn in the lock.

She stood listening and knew that for the
moment Major Meredith did not move.
Then she heard his footsteps going away

down the passage and sank down onto her bunk.

He had apologised for one thing and she wished with a kind of fervour that could not be repressed that she could tell him how wrong he had been in his suppositions when he had seen her in Queen Anne Street.

'He will never know the truth,' she told herself aloud and could not help hearing the note of despair in her voice.

The following day a breeze sprang up at dawn and the ship's sails carried them forward at a greater speed than they had attained for the last forty-eight hours.

"We should be in Bombay on time," the General said when Orissa took Neil to see his grandparents in the morning after breakfast.

It was so hot that she had put on one of the pretty new muslin dresses she had made herself. She was well aware that it became her and she looked very fresh and young in the sunshine.

"You must be looking forward to seeing your husband again, Mrs. Lane," Lady Critchley remarked.

"Yes, of . . . course," Orissa replied.

"He will be meeting you at Bombay?"

"I . . . expect so," she answered.

131

"Then we must not forget to thank you for what you have done for little Neil," Lady Critchley said. "He certainly looks better since he has been in your care."

"Thank you," Orissa said, surprised at Lady Critchley's gratitude.

She took Neil's hand to take him for a walk round the deck and before she was out of ear-shot she heard Lady Critchley say to the General:

"That is a very well-behaved young woman."

Orissa could not help thinking with a wry smile, it was a pity that Major Meredith could not hear Lady Critchley's remark.

Then she thought with amusement how horrified Her Ladyship would be if she had any idea of how the Major had behaved.

'It is a good thing they cannot thought-read,' she told herself, and forced her thoughts away from Major Meredith to concentrate on amusing Neil.

Although she felt inclined as it was growing near the end of the voyage to relax her rule of having dinner alone, she decided it would be impossible to encounter Major Meredith with an indifferent composure or indeed to bear the scrutiny of his grey eyes.

He would never learn how grossly he had misjudged her, and she could not help wondering whether, if they had met in different circumstances, he would still have wished to kiss her.

Had his action the night he had taken her in his arms under the stars been merely that of a man seeking amusement because it was easy and he did not have to exert himself to find it?

Or had he any different or perhaps deeper feelings where she was concerned?

That was a question to which she would never know the answer, Orissa realised despairingly and wondered because she could not help it, if he had ever wished to kiss her again.

Even to think of it was to know that strange happiness of feeling secure and to relive the ecstasy which had made her whole body quiver.

Had that moment of rapture, that moment of glory, been only too commonplace where he was concerned?

Had she been just another woman whose lips he had sought? Just a female whose body perhaps attracted him fleetingly and whom he would forget the moment he set foot on dry land?

She could not understand why the idea made her feel so despondent; why, despite the fact that she hated him for his suspicions and the manner in which he had behaved, she wanted him to remember her.

'My first kiss,' Orissa told herself.

She had an uncomfortable feeling that never again would anybody be able to evoke in her anything quite so exquisite, so breath-takingly wonderful.

It was the last night on board that she came face to face with Major Meredith walking down the passageway towards her cabin.

She had been to the Purser's office after dinner to collect some labels for the baggage.

She was sure that everyone else was in the Dining-Hall and that she would not be seen.

She had dined alone as usual and thought that at least after tomorrow there would be fresh food — fruit picked from the trees that morning, and meat and fish that had not been frozen.

However skilfully cooked there was a sameness about the taste of food which had been refrigerated and which no sauce or gravy could disguise.

Because it was very hot and because all her things were packed, Orissa was wearing only a thin muslin day-dress and her hair was caught up into a big, loose chignon at the back of her head.

"Tomorrow you will see Mama," she had said to Neil as she put him to bed.

He had gone to sleep clutching his painting-book because he was so frightened he would lose it before he could give it to his mother.

'It seems strange,' Orissa thought to herself, 'that in some ways the ship has become so familiar during the voyage that it is like leaving a house that has been a home.'

She had grown used to the routine: to the Stewards, to the Purser and the passengers she met every day.

She had even grown to like some of those who always talked to Neil and to herself as they moved around the deck. She knew they were curious about her and would have questioned her closely if she had allowed them to do so.

After tomorrow she would never see any of them again. They were just "ships that pass in the night" and as easily forgotten.

'With the exception of one,' her brain said firmly.

It was true, Orissa thought, she would never be able to forget Major Meredith.

They would never meet again, but he had done something that she could never erase from her memory.

He had kissed her!

He was the first man to do so — the only man! She had the uneasy feeling that she would always compare what she felt when his lips touched hers with any kiss that she received in the future.

As Orissa walked down the corridor and saw Major Meredith coming towards her her heart gave a sudden, unexpected leap. It was almost as if it turned over in her breast and it was hard to breathe.

'I do not wish to speak to him,' she thought suddenly panic-stricken, but it was too late to do anything about it.

"I was hoping to see you, Mrs. Lane," Major Meredith remarked.

He came to a stop when he reached her and stood so that it was impossible for her to pass by him without having to push him aside.

Orissa raised her eyes to his face but she did not speak.

"Your husband will I presume, be meeting you at Bombay."

"I hope . . . so," Orissa managed to answer.

"Is there anything I can do to help you after we have disembarked?"

"No, thank you. There is nothing."

Their words were conventional, spoken in low voices that seemed deliberately devoid of expression and yet, Orissa thought wildly, there was so much left unsaid.

She had a sudden crazy impulse to move towards him; to touch him; to ask him to kiss her just once more.

She wanted to be sure that she had not been dreaming or imagining the emotions he aroused in her that night under the stars. Then she told herself that he must not despise her more than he did already.

With an effort that was almost painful because she had to force it upon herself, she put out her hand.

"Good-bye, Major Meredith."

She felt the hard strength of his fingers and somehow it made her quiver.

"Good-bye, Mrs. Lane. I hope you will be as happy in India as you expect to be."

"Thank you."

She thought he would never relinquish her hand. She did not dare look into his eyes.

Then she was free. He was walking away from her down the passage and she felt inexplicably that he was taking with him something of herself.

CHAPTER FIVE

The bustle and noise on the quay was almost deafening.

The passengers coming down the First Class gangway seemed to be plunged into a maelstrom of dark bodies, baggage and bales, children screaming, men shouting and an indescribable general confusion from which one felt that nothing could emerge but chaos.

Orissa's steward who had found a coolie to take her luggage waited for her to give him instructions.

She had expected only half-heartedly that there would be someone to meet her. She hoped perhaps her Uncle might have instructed a friend or one of his officers in Bombay to be on the quay when the ship docked.

Then she told herself it was far more likely that he would meet her at Delhi.

After all, if Charles had telegraphed him

as they had arranged he would be sure that she would be chaperoned on the voyage and that whoever was looking after her would see her into the train for Delhi.

Nevertheless she stood for a moment in the seething crowd wondering if there was anyone looking for her and hoping they would not miss her.

The coolie, half naked and with ragged clothing waited philosophically for her to make up her mind as to where he was to take her baggage.

There was not much of it and she was thankful that she had not, like most of the other passengers, to wait until the luggage which had been in the hold came ashore.

She had forgotten, she thought, how overwhelming the crowds could be in India, and yet even in this moment of confusion her heart leaped at the colour that was everywhere.

There were Indians waiting with garlands of marigolds for their friends to disembark from the ship and the brilliance of the saris seemed to be echoed in the uniforms of the various soldiers of all ranks moving about the quayside.

There were vendors selling fruits of green, purple and orange. There were children of well-off Indians carrying coloured windmills and kites, and everywhere there were beautiful faces with huge brown liquid eyes.

And above all there was the sunshine, golden and warm which penetrated even through the covered part of the quay and enveloped the ship Orissa had just left in a kind of golden haze.

"Is anyone meeting you, Mrs. Lane?"

She had no need to turn her head to see who had asked her the question in his deep voice.

As if she had half-anticipated that Major Meredith would find her again even though she had said good-bye to him, a lie sprang to her lips.

"A carriage will be . . . waiting for me . . . outside."

"Then shall I tell your porter to take you there?"

"Thank you, that would be very kind."

Orissa managed to speak with a cold reserve.

She had the uncomfortable feeling that Major Meredith was trying to find out more about her; perhaps to meet her mythical husband, or even to make sure that she was in fact not left alone in Bombay.

She had said good-bye to the General and Lady Critchley on board and the latter had actually had a note of warmth in her voice when she thanked Orissa for all she had done for little Neil.

Neil's mother, who had met her father and mother before they had disembarked, had been most effusive.

"I cannot be too grateful to you, Mrs. Lane," she said, "Mama tells me that you have improved Neil's health and made him behave like an angel throughout the whole voyage."

"He is a dear little boy," Orissa said affectionately.

"Have you any children of your own?"

"No."

"I felt you must have," Neil's mother smiled, "to have been so clever with mine. But thank you — thank you more than I can say."

"It has been a very great pleasure!" Orissa replied.

Then a number of smart be-medalled officers appeared, to escort the General to his carriage and Orissa slipped away.

She had expected that Major Meredith also would have a welcoming party awaiting him, but he appeared to be alone.

For one uncomfortable moment she thought that he intended to come with her and her coolie in search of the carriage which she had said was outside.

Firmly she held her hand out to him.

"Good-bye, Major Meredith."

"Perhaps we shall meet again," he suggested. "I am often in Bombay."

"I think it is unlikely," Orissa replied.

She felt this was unnecessarily rude and as an afterthought added:

"My . . . husband and I do not . . . entertain very much."

"Then I must not try to impose on your hospitality," Major Meredith said.

And she knew by the twist of his lips that he realised she was trying to be rid of him.

At that moment a truck containing a great pile of baggage from the ship pushed passed them amid cries from the porters to clear the way, and Orissa turned and followed her own small pile of luggage without another look at Major Meredith.

'I really shall never see him again,' she told herself and wondered why the thought gave her so little pleasure.

Outside a number of *gharri-wallahs* — the cab-drivers of hired carriages, solicited her custom for their shabby gharris.

Her coolie chose one and having piled the baggage on the seat opposite her thanked her for the tip she gave him.

"Where Mem-sahib go?" the *gharri-wallah* enquired.

"The Victoria Terminus," Orissa instructed him, "but drive round by the sea."

She had been to Bombay before, but it seemed to her that it had grown tremendously in the eight years since she had been in India.

There was still the beautiful bay shimmering in the heat so that it gave the illusion of being hardly real.

The enormous group of official buildings to which Orissa was sure a great many had been added, stood like a massive palisade parallel with the sea, separated from the beaches by an expanse of brownish turf, a railway line and a riding-track which she remembered was called "Rotten Row".

She recognised some of the buildings as ones she had seen before. Many were Venetian Gothic, some decorated in French fashion, others early English, while the Post Office was simply pseudo-mediaeval.

Enormous palm-mat awnings shaded the windows and there were white-suited figures strolling high on the balconies, while below them were the teaming crowds of dark-skinned figures.

There were stalls piled high with water-melons or vividly coloured glass bowls with drinks so cheap that even the poorest could afford to buy one.

There were men selling sweet-meats or tobacco, chapattis or fruit, and cakes fried in fat.

It was all so familiar; the bustling and shouting, the creaking of wagon-wheels, the bullocks drawing great loads, and the veiled women wearing yashmaks or their voluminous enveloping *bourgas* pulled closely about their faces.

To Orissa it was part of her childhood, and all too quickly the *gharri-wallah* brought her to the Victoria Terminus, where there were still more crowds and the Station was so full there was hardly room to move.

A stranger might have been under the impression that a Festival was taking place or that there was some special reason for such a crowd to have congregated at the Terminus.

But Orissa knew from the past that a Hindu, having asked the price of the ticket to where he is to travel, will seldom ask the time of the departure of the train.

When the day of his journey drew near, he would move into the Station with his family.

They spread their sleeping-mats on the platform, cooked their food over small braziers, washed under the Station tap while the railway officials, luggage coolies and passengers step over and around them.

Orissa went to the ticket office and was forced to wait for some time because of several fierce arguments between would-be passengers and the official selling tickets.

"A first class ticket to Delhi, please," she said, "and what time does the next train leave?"

She learned that she had missed the morning train which was the fastest of the day and must now wait until the evening.

The wait would not be arduous. She could buy food and there was much to amuse her.

The porter who had taken her luggage from the *gharri* was quite prepared to do nothing else but watch it and she sat down on a seat enjoying the scene in front of her.

There were not only people to watch, but goats and chickens, pai-dogs running about apparently, unattended, and even a sacred white Brahmini bull which had apparently got in by mistake!

She refused offers of curry, savoury hot food and a glass of sherbet, but she did accept a green coconut, off which the seller obligingly hacked the top, so that she could drink the cool milk.

She was thirsty because it was very hot but she knew that she must not drink the water and she did not fancy the cups which the *chai-wallah* offered her filled with hot tea.

There were many other things to see as well: barrows laden with toys, baskets of wooden animals and birds painted with crimson daisies and yellow roses. There were palm-leaf fans so cheap that Orissa allowed herself the luxury of one.

When at last in the late afternoon the train did arrive, puffing and blowing like some fierce dragon descending menacingly upon the crowded Station, the noise was indescribable.

Those asleep on the platform sprang to life and the Station was filled with an unearthly clamour.

The loud orders of native policemen who had suddenly appeared from no-where mingled with the shrill yells of women gathering up their children, their animals and their husbands.

Orissa's porter found her a first class carriage marked 'Ladies Only'. He reserved her a corner seat before anyone else could enter and heaved her luggage up onto the rack.

He was so delighted with what she gave him for his trouble, that she knew that she must have over-tipped him.

But she told herself that it did not matter.

She had plenty of money left.

When she left the ship the General had tipped the Steward who looked after the State-room which she and Neil occupied. So apart from her lessons with Mr. Mahla she had in fact incurred no expenses while she had been on board.

The first class fare to Delhi had not been cheap, but Uncle Henry was waiting at the other end, and she thought with satisfaction that the money that Charles had given her would come in very useful in refurbishing her wardrobe.

She was well aware that she would need many more dresses if she was to do her Uncle credit and perhaps play Hostess for him.

When they went further North with the Regiment in perhaps a month's time, there would be no need for her to look quite so smart.

But Delhi would be full of Officers' wives, and she was well aware that the searching eye of a female would quickly perceive how worn her clothes really were.

Nevertheless she had her pretty new muslin dresses to wear and at least two evening gowns of which she was not completely ashamed.

'I will go to the native Bazaar,' she told

herself. 'I can buy really cheap materials and far better than those in the shops which cater for the white population.'

The carriage soon filled up.

There were three officers' wives, but their husbands belonged to different Regiments so they were politely cool with each other showing a British reserve which Orissa found amusing.

There was a gaunt-faced missionary who sat in the corner reading tracts and speaking to no-one.

There was a plump little woman — obviously the wife of a business man — who settled herself comfortably as soon as she got in, closed her eyes and prepared to sleep.

The officers' wives glanced at Orissa from under their eyelashes but made no attempt to get into conversation with her. She was glad because when the train started she wanted to watch the country speeding by until it grew dark.

They stopped after two hours and everyone surged onto the platform in search of food.

Orissa by this time felt hungry and she bought herself a hard-boiled egg, two large chapatti and some fruit, avoiding the expensive English food in the Station buffet.

Soon after the train started off again it

was dark, and the ladies producing pillows, rugs and blankets all settled themselves down to sleep.

Orissa made herself as comfortable as she could, but the noise of the train and the way it jerked nearly to a standstill and then accelerated back to its previous speed was not restful.

Although the windows were shut the dust penetrated and threw a thin grey film over them all, so that at the frequent stops it seemed to Orissa more important to wash than to bother about food.

She did however walk up the train at one stop and found there were a number of horses on the train from the famous Arab stables at Bombay.

She knew that one of the sights of Bombay was the Bendhi bazaar where the dealers from the Persian Gulf sold their horses.

The Indian Army was a great market for Arab horses, and Orissa wished she could see the arch-necked animals that were being carried to Delhi to join the others of their kind that were so important a part of the Indian Cavalry Regiments.

It was exciting to think that once she was with her Uncle she would be able to ride again. As she thought of it she wondered what Major Meredith looked like on a horse.

She had the feeling, though she could not think why, that he was an exceptional horseman.

There was something about his hands, she thought, that told her he would handle an animal gently, but at the same time so firmly there would be no mistaking who was master.

Sitting in the train she shut her eyes and tried to go to sleep, but she found herself thinking of that night when looking out over the desert, she had spoken of loneliness and Major Meredith had kissed her.

He had done it, she must suppose, mockingly, and yet she could still remember the sense of security his arms had given her.

He had held her again as he carried her up the stairs to the Writing-room when she had nearly fainted.

Even then she had known the same extraordinary feeling of safety.

'I shall never see him again,' Orissa told herself. 'It was just an episode in my life and the sooner I can forget it the better.'

But she could not forget the feelings Major Meredith had evoked in her with his lips.

The train sped on, stopped and started again for two nights and a day until finally they reached Delhi.

The light after the darkness seemed almost blinding and as they drew near the City Orissa had a glimpse of a tall, Gothic spire, memorial to the British dead in the Mutiny on the ridge.

But she remembered that the city had been for nearly one thousand years one of the great historic capitals of Asia.

She longed to see again the fabulous Red Fort to which she had been taken as a child.

She could recall its red bricks glowing like rubies and how it had been built by Shah Jahan who had designed the Taj Mahal, the most romantic building in the world, in memory of his wife.

He mourned her for thirty-six years after she died, Orissa remembered.

'If only I could be loved like that!'

Then because she knew it would never happen, she forced herself to think about Delhi.

'I shall be able to explore the whole city while Uncle Henry is here,' she thought excitedly.

She tidied herself before the train drew into the Station.

Fortunately the muslin dress had creased very little during the journey and she tried to brush away the dust from her dark hair before she put on a small cheap chip-straw bonnet which was the only summer hat she possessed.

The officers' wives stepped out of the carriage first. There were three tall, bronzed men to meet them, smart and spruce in their uniforms and giving sharp orders to the coolie-boys to collect luggage.

The missionary swept away without a good-bye, and the fat woman who appeared still to be sleepy was met by a Bearer who escorted her away with an officious air which told Orissa that the lady was of more importance than she had suspected.

She stepped out at last onto the platform and looked around her.

The crowds were thick, but the first class carriages were all in one section of the train, and anyone meeting her would know where to wait.

If her Uncle could not come himself she was certain he would send one of his officers.

She waited but no-one spoke to her, except coolies asking if they could carry her luggage.

Finally, because she was afraid the train might pull out of the Station, she instructed one to lift her baggage down from the rack.

He put it beside her on the platform and again she waited until at last she realised that once again Charles's memory had failed.

He must have forgotten to send her Uncle a telegram and now she would arrive unannounced and unexpected.

'Really, it is too bad of him!' she murmured to herself.

But she knew that she had really suspected he had forgotten when there had been no-one to greet her at Bombay.

The trouble was that she did not know the name of the Barracks where the Regiment was stationed, having omitted to ask Charles such an important detail.

There were so many soldiers in Delhi and it was quite likely there would be more than one Barracks.

Then she told herself that all she had to do was to find someone British who could tell her where the Chilterns were stationed.

There were always officers on duty at Railway Stations. It would be easy to obtain such information. There was certainly enough military personnel about.

She could see in the crowds Sikhs from the North with brilliant turbans, beards and long moustaches, Pathan warriors from the North-West Frontier, the uniforms of the 21st Bengal Native Infantry and the Madras Cavalry.

Each man was distinctive in himself, yet they all fused into a harmonious whole, from the stalwarts of the Rajput states to the Sikhims and Bhutans with a Mongol slant to their eyes, and the exquisitely fragile Dravidians from the south.

Then as Orissa pushed her way towards the railway offices followed by her coolie carrying her baggage, she saw the uniform of the Royal Chilterns.

It was worn by a Sikh, a magnificent man carrying himself with a pride that was a part of his noble history, his dark beard curling round his chin, his full eyebrows almost meeting across his hooked nose.

Eagerly Orissa went up to him.

"Have you been sent to meet me, Sergeant-Major? I am Lady Orissa Fane."

The Sergeant Major saluted her smartly.

"I'm waiting for a train, Mem-Sahib."

"Then tell me," Orissa said, "where in Delhi can I find Colonel Henry Hobart?"

"Colonel not in Delhi, Mem-Sahib."

"Not in Delhi?" Orissa exclaimed in dismay, "but I am his niece. I have come from England to stay with him."

"Colonel Sahib and battalion of the Regiment sent Shuba, Mem-Sahib."

As if he saw by Orissa's expression that

154

she did not know where Shuba was, he explained:

"Shuba on the Frontier, Mem-Sahib, beyond Peshawar. Talk of trouble. They left a week ago. I go now join them."

Orissa stood staring at him in perplexity.

That Uncle Henry should not be in Delhi was something that she had not contemplated for a moment.

Charles had said that they were to be stationed there for at least two months, and even deducting time spent on her journey from England, that should have given her over a month's grace.

She wondered desperately what she should do. She knew there must be officers' wives to whom she could appeal. The Commander-in-Chief, who had a house in Delhi, would obviously advise her where she could stay until her Uncle's return.

Then she realised how embarrassing it would be to have to explain why she had come to India at a moment's notice, and without even warning her Uncle of her arrival.

She could imagine the curiosity of the women. She could imagine how hard it would be to explain away the fact that she had travelled without a chaperon.

How could she say?:

"I pretended to be a married woman."

And if she told the truth she knew how quickly news travelled in India, and it would be only a question of time before the General and Lady Critchley learnt how she had deceived them.

She felt everything going round in her mind like the jingling music of a hurdy-gurdy.

And then she said to the waiting Sikh:

"Did you say, Sergeant Major, that you were joining my Uncle?"

"Yes, Mem-Sahib, I been ill with denghi fever. Colonel Sahib instruct me join him soon as I better."

"Then I will come with you," Orissa said.

"With me, Mem-Sahib?"

"Yes," Orissa answered firmly. "You will take me to the Colonel, Sergeant Major. He must have left before the telegram arrived to inform him of my coming, otherwise he would doubtless have left someone here to look after me."

"But, Mem-Sahib . . ." the Sergeant Major began.

"There is nothing else I can do," Orissa interrupted, "and I know that the Colonel would not wish me left alone in Delhi. You can understand that."

"Yes, indeed, Mem-Sahib, but surely

ladies — friends of Colonel-Sahib would look after you?"

"I have to be with my Uncle," Orissa said firmly. "It is very important, you understand, that I should reach him as soon as possible. What time does the train for Shuba leave?"

"In one hour, Mem-Sahib."

"Very well," Orissa said, "you will get me a ticket."

She took out her purse as she spoke, then hesitated.

She was well aware it would not be cheap to travel to Shuba. It was a long way from Delhi.

"I am travelling second class, Sergeant Major."

"Second class, Mem-Sahib?" he queried in surprise.

Orissa of course knew that the British gentry travelled first class in India, usually with a servant's compartment next door. On some railways a little window linked them through which the Sahib could give orders.

The Indian gentry travelled second class, the British "other ranks", industrial and commercial men, went Intermediate, whilst squeezed, squashed, levered and pushed into the slatted wooden seats of the fourth class compartments travelled the ordinary Indians.

Journeys took a long time and the Sahibs took their own padded quilts and pillows with them, and always their own "tiffin-basket".

When Orissa had travelled with her father he used to telegraph his requirements ahead, and as the train drew into the Station, out of the shadows would step a man in white carrying food on a tray covered with a napkin.

She could remember fiery curry which even when she was young she had not found too hot, and to wash it down there had been lemonade in the tiffin-basket for her and whisky for her father.

Now, Orissa thought, she dared not expend her precious money in case when she reached Shuba she could not afford to go any further.

She was not certain where Shuba was, but doubtless she would have to pay for a carriage on arrival.

"I will travel second class," she said firmly, and handed the Sergeant Major her purse.

She had no hesitation in doing that; for an Indian who had reached the rank of Sergeant Major would be scrupulously honest and would never rob his employers, with the exception of the small bucksheesh to which he was entitled on every purchase.

She then went to the comfortable Ladies Waiting-room where she found it possible to wash herself thoroughly and to rid her hair of the dust that had accumulated on the train from Bombay.

She was quite certain that the dust would be far worse on the Punjab Northern State Railway on which she was to travel now — but at least she would start clean!

When she came back onto the platform, it was to find the Sergeant Major waiting with her ticket, and looking so smart and authoritative that she was glad to have him with her.

She was half afraid that some officious British Railway Officer would enquire where she was going and why she was travelling alone, but when escorted by the Sergeant Major, Orissa knew she would arouse no curiosity.

The train came in on time and once again there was the same confusion, noise and frenzy that had taken place at Bombay.

British passengers in spotless white stalked the platform in a miasma of privilege, followed by convoys of servants and porters with bags and children, bedding and tennis-rackets, polo-sticks and cricket bats.

It was a kaleidoscope of colour with turbans of every hue from pale pink to vermillion, scarlet uniforms, yellow priestly robes, and strangely hued loin-cloths.

Finally the travellers got aboard and once again Orissa found herself a corner seat, but this time the cushions were not so comfortable, there was less space and more people in the compartment.

They were all Indians with the exception of herself.

Opposite her was a pretty little woman expensively bejewelled whom Orissa judged to be a Parsee.

Indian women always travel wearing their jewellery because they have nowhere to leave it when they are away from home.

The Parsee had flashing ear-rings, a profusion of golden bracelets, a necklace set with rubies and diamonds and several rings on her thin, artistic fingers.

Parsees were easy to distinguish. Followers of the Prophet Zoroaster, they were descendants of the Persians who emigrated to India to avoid religious persecution by the Moslems.

They had as a race grown very rich and mostly lived in Bombay, where the British complained they owned so many grand houses that it was impossible to compete with them!

The Parsee had a great number of suitcases and as the train started she tried to arrange them more securely on the rack and in doing so stood on the hem of her rose-pink Sari and tore it.

She gave an exclamation of annoyance and Orissa said in Urdu:

"What a pity as your sari is so pretty! Let me mend it for you."

The Parsee looked at her in surprise. Then as Orissa searched in one of her bags for her sewing materials the whole carriage began to discuss the slight mishap.

It was disgraceful, they said, how badly the coolies put the luggage on the racks; the racks were too high; it was impossible to expect a woman to lift down such heavy objects and anyway the train only catered for men!

Everybody enjoyed expressing their views, and it was so unlike the austere silence in which Orissa had travelled from Bombay to Delhi with the English ladies.

She skilfully repaired the sari with such fine stitches that it was impossible when she had finished to see where the tear had been.

"You are very gracious," the Parsee exclaimed.

"It is nothing," Orissa smiled, and soon they were all talking.

They talked about their children, their husbands, their difficulties in finding materials and the household appliances they wanted, the heat, the lack of water, their fears and frustrations, travel and every other subject which came into their heads — talking quickly in their sing-song voices.

They sounded like little birds in a cage making music.

Orissa learnt that the Parsee was the only one who could speak any English.

"I have a shop," she explained to Orissa. "My customers are mostly rich Indian ladies, but sometimes the English memsahibs patronise me as well. They buy saris to take home to their friends."

"We have nothing so beautiful in England," Orissa said with a smile.

"Your gown is very beautiful," the Parsee said in obvious sincerity.

"I made it myself," Orissa explained.

There was a great deal of excitement over this, and the other ladies in the carriage asked her to stand up so that they could admire the bustle and they fingered the material. They paid her compliments. It was all very amusing and feminine.

Orissa had planned to alight at the first

stop to buy some food but the Parsee and the others would not hear of such a thing. They shared curries and chapattis with her and the other food they had brought with them and Orissa found it delicious.

The Sergeant-Major came to the window of the carriage to see if there was anything she required.

On Orissa's instructions he bought her fruit — oranges and sweet melons which she shared with the other members of the compartment feeling she should make her contribution to the general feast.

She was well aware that many Indians would have felt that for her to share their meal would be sacrilege. But there appeared to be a camaraderie between them because she had been friendly, which overrode the taboos of caste.

The train moved off again and soon they were ready to settle down for the night.

The carriage was less crowded now as three of the women had alighted and Orissa realised she could get her feet up on the seat next to her and rest more comfortably.

The Parsee took off her fine, gold-embroidered sari to put on a plainer, less expensive one.

"It will be hot to-night," she said to Orissa. "You will find it difficult to sleep in your pretty gown. Would you permit me to lend you a sari? That is if you would condescend to accept one from me."

"Do you really mean that?" Orissa asked. "It is very kind of you."

"I should be honoured," the Parsee answered.

The whole carriage was amused and interested at seeing Orissa undress. They exclaimed over her petticoats, were entranced by the small tight corset which pulled in her waist, the strange shape of her lace-edged drawers, and her thin chemise.

They modestly looked the other way when Orissa put on the short low-necked bodice which every Indian woman wears. She caught the sari around her waist and flung it over one shoulder delighted that she had not forgotten how to arrange it.

The ladies exclaimed with delight at her appearance.

"You might be one of us!" one of the women exclaimed and it was meant to be a compliment.

Orissa remembered that Charles had said she looked like a Rajput Princess. As she studied herself in the mirror which the Parsee produced from her luggage she thought he was right!

She not only felt far more comfortable but

far more attractive as well.

The sari, which was a deep, ruby red, threw into prominence the darkness of her hair with its faint blue lights. She might in fact easily have come from one of the Northern Provinces where neither the men's nor women's skins were as dark as those in the South.

With no constricting corset round her waist it was easy to curl up on the seat and sleep.

One of the ladies loaned her a rolled-up blanket to use as a pillow, and because she had been awake nearly the whole of the night before Orissa fell into a dreamless slumber.

She awakened to find the dawn light streaming in through the windows and showing up the amount of dust that had accumulated on the floor during the night.

Her fellow passengers were all still asleep. They had pulled their saris over their heads and they looked, lying in the seats, more like colourful bundles than women.

Orissa had only been awake for a few moments when the train came to a halt. It was not a big Station, but even so early in the morning there was a large crowd.

The sellers were there to hawk their wares, and after a few seconds the Sergeant-Major came to the window of the carriage.

He looked in and Orissa saw a look of consternation on his face. He looked from one side of the compartment to the other, then took two steps back on the platform to make sure he had the right carriage and then came to look in again.

Orissa bent forward.

"You did not recognise me, Sergeant-Major?" she asked.

"Mem-Sahib!" he exclaimed in surprise.

"I am far more comfortable in these clothes," Orissa explained.

"There is something I must say to you, Mem-Sahib," he said in a low voice. "It is important."

He opened the door and Orissa stepped out on to the platform.

They walked a little way from the crowds and standing beside a wall covered with instructions in two languages Orissa asked:

"What is it?"

She felt something had gone wrong.

"You not, Mem-Sahib, go any further than Peshawar," the Sergeant-Major said, "I speak with the officers on train. They say big trouble at the frontier, that why Colonel Sahib sent to Shuba."

"Worse trouble than usual?" Orissa asked.

"Yes, Mem-Sahib. Talk of Russians over

166

border stirring up tribesmen."

Orissa was silent, and then the Sergeant-Major said:

"I think, Mem-Sahib, when we reach Peshawar British Officials make you return to Delhi. You not allowed proceed with me."

"I must get to my Uncle, I must!"

Then an idea came to her.

"Listen, Sergeant-Major. When I am dressed like this, would you know I was English?"

"No, Mem-Sahib, if you have caste-mark you look like Hindu lady."

"Then, Sergeant-Major, when we get to Peshawar, you will not be escorting an English lady, but one of your own family, your sister perhaps?"

The Sergeant-Major look at her speculatively.

"No-one ask questions, Mem-Sahib," he said at last positively.

"How were you intending that we should reach Shuba?" Orissa asked.

'I hire *gharri* for you, Mem-Sahib. Now unlikely *gharri-wallah,* who are cowardly, fearful chaps, would make journey."

"And how would you get there?"

"March, Mem-Sahib."

"How far is it?"

"Twenty miles."

Orissa gave a little sigh.

She was well aware as an Indian she would not wear stout, walking shoes on her feet but sandals.

"Not worry, Mem-Sahib," the Sergeant-Major said quickly, "I find way of getting you to Shuba. Colonel Sahib not wish you return alone to Delhi."

"I am quite sure my Uncle would not wish that," Orissa agreed. "Wait a minute while I get you my purse. If I were an Indian lady I would certainly not be carrying my own money if there was a man to look after me."

She went back to the carriage and found the purse which the Sergeant-Major had given back to her after he had purchased her ticket.

She put it into his hands.

"We reach Peshawar in one hour, Mem-Sahib," he said in a low voice and left her.

Orissa got back into the carriage and when the train started she said in English to the Parsee who was by now awake:

"I want to speak to you but I do not want the others to understand."

"Speak slowly," the Parsee admonished.

"I have to reach my Uncle, who is the Colonel of the Royal Chilterns," Orissa explained, "but the Sergeant-Major thinks as these are troublesome times it will be wiser for me to go dressed as I am now. May I therefore ask you a great favour?"

Her voice was rather embarrassed, but she continued:

"May I keep the sari you have so kindly loaned me? I promise to pay the full cost of it to your address in Bombay as soon as I reach my Uncle. I swear that I will not cheat you."

"But of course you must not pay! I should not think of such a thing from a lady such as you. I give it to you. It is a gift!"

"No, no, I cannot accept!" Orissa expostulated.

They argued for fully ten minutes before Orissa realised that the Parsee really wished her to take the sari as a present and would only accept in return a pair of white kid-gloves which Orissa had in her baggage.

"It is a good exchange," the Parsee said. "I cannot buy such gloves in India."

Orissa then explained that she would be deeply grateful if she could also borrow a little henna for her hands and the paint for a red caste-mark on her forehead.

By now the other ladies of the carriage had been let into the secret, although Orissa was careful not to tell them her ultimate destination.

They produced not only henna but khol

for her eyes, and they even insisted on giving her some glass bracelets to wear around her wrists.

"All Indian women wear jewellery," they said. "You would appear very poor with a very stingy husband not to possess any ornaments."

Orissa protested she could not accept such generosity but it all became a game. Her hands, her nails and her feet were hennaed, her eyes made dark and beguiling as any Oriental woman, there was a crimson caste-mark in the centre of her forehead.

She had little she could give in return. A piece of the ribbon left over from decorating her green dress, half a yard of tulle and besides the gloves for the Parsee who had given her the sari, two little lace-edged handkerchiefs she had made herself.

It was a poor exchange, but she felt she had provided the Indian women with so much to talk about and think about that it was in itself adequate recompense.

The train was slowing down and Orissa realised they were drawing into Peshawar which was the end of the line.

She felt a sudden tremor of excitement.

'Now I really am embarking on a great adventure!' she told herself.

CHAPTER SIX

When Orissa saw the *tika-gharri* which the Sergeant-Major brought to the station for her she wanted to laugh aloud.

There was nothing funnier than a native cart which looked like a box on wheels, and which in fact it actually was!

There was a flat piece of wood fastened overhead to serve as protection from the sun and there was only just room enough for two people to sit inside and very little space indeed for any baggage.

The Sergeant-Major had warned Orissa of this before he went in search of a vehicle to convey them to Shuba.

He left Orissa at the station telling her that when he returned he would convey most of her luggage to an office where it would be safe until it could be collected.

"If all well, Mem-Sahib," he said, "brake can be sent from Fort to carry bags. But Indian ladies travel light."

Orissa took the hint and finding a corner in the waiting-room used by Indian women and not English ladies, she unpacked and repacked all she thought she would need.

This required a large holdall made of canvas which she had brought with her from London to hold books and other small items which might be needed on the voyage.

She thought she must have two of her muslin day-gowns and one for the evening with her, as she was sure that her Uncle would not wish her to walk about the Fort dressed in a sari!

Knowing also that the weather in the North-West Provinces would be cool at night she put in a warmer wrap than she would have needed in any other part of India.

The canvas bag had eventually to be strapped to hold it together, but small though it seemed to her she thought the Sergeant-Major looked at it somewhat disapprovingly when he returned to the station.

He made no comment however and collecting a coolie had Orissa's round-topped leather trunks taken to an office.

Keeping well in the background, Orissa heard the Sergeant-Major explain that her luggage must be kept with the greatest care and in complete safety until the Colonel Henry Hobart of the Royal Chilterns could send for it.

It was obvious that her Uncle's name commanded respect, and the Sergeant-Major was given a receipt signed by a Senior Official.

Saluting smartly the Sergeant-Major marched away without a glance at Orissa who followed behind him in subservient Eastern fashion.

Outside the station the *tika-gharri* was waiting in the charge of a small, ragged boy.

It was obviously old and weather-beaten, the original blue with which it had been painted had faded and there were several cracks in the wooden sides.

At the same time the wheels looked strong and the thin dun-coloured horse which pulled it had, Orissa hoped, more stamina than its appearance suggested.

She was however well aware that the slim-legged but sure-footed Northern horses were strong and reliable when it came to long distances and mountain roads.

She was certain that the Sergeant-Major would not have been deceived in any animal he had hired.

Her canvas bag was disposed of under the hard wooden seat and she climbed into the *tika-gharri.* The ragged boy was rewarded with a small coin and they set off to drive through the town.

There were numerous soldiers to be seen in uniform, but not a sign of any British women, which made Orissa feel sure that the Sergeant-Major had been right when he said that if any of the officials had known who she was she would have been compelled to return to Delhi.

She looked around her with curiosity and excitement, remembering to keep her sari pulled well over her forehead and to hold it sideways across her face so that only her kohl-ringed eyes could be seen by those who looked in her direction.

Peshawar had been founded in the 16th Century by the Mongul Emperor Akbar, lying only 18 miles from the Khyber Pass.

Two years earlier a further extension of the Punjab Northern State Railway had been completed joining the old city to the British Civil Station and Cantonment two miles to the West.

Shuba however lay to the East and therefore could not be reached by road. The *tika-gharri* moved through the crowds towards the Northern Gate.

Orissa had a look at the new factories as she passed. Peshawar was famous for its manufacture of woollen cloths, silks and above all carpets.

These were woven by men with shaved heads wearing "durees" who had been sentenced to prison.

"Many of the prisoners are Afreedies, bad men," the Sergeant-Major told her.

Orissa remembered that the wild habits of the Afreedies had caused the Punjab Government a lot of trouble.

She looked with affection at the Pathans who strode the street.

Her father had often quoted:

"Trust a Brahmin before a snake, and a snake before a harlot, and a harlot before a Pathan."

But she had known them all her childhood and she loved the most ferocious, independent, and warlike race the world had ever known.

Divided into dozens of tribes, the Pathans looked on King Saul as their ancestor, but had been converted to Islam.

Some Pathans were light of skin, eyes and hair, many had aquiline noses, a rosy white complexion, nut brown eyes and hair, others had broad high cheek-boned faces.

Orissa knew that whatever their strain, all Pathans were reserved and proud, and were bound by their traditions to exact vengeance

175

for any wrong — actual or fancied. This alone made the Frontier one of the most sensitive and explosive areas on earth.

She spoke of this to the Sergeant-Major and he replied curtly:

"Most grievances come from Zar, Zan and Zamin."

Orissa knew that this meant — "Gold, women and land."

She also saw in the crowded streets an Akali, a wild-haired, wild-eyed Sikh, in the blue-checked clothes of his faith, with polished steel quoits glistening on the cone of his tall, blue turban.

There were women with babies on their hips who all wore the dull, glass bracelets made in the North West.

There was a gang of Changars — the women who work on the embankments of all the Northern railways — big-bosomed, flat-footed and strong-limbed. They, as Orissa knew, were the earth-carriers and had a strength that was proverbial in a land of delicate, fragile women.

The town of Peshawar seemed prosperous, as towns always were when there were troops with money to spend.

The cloth shops were inviting with rolls of cloth laid on shelves open to the street and gay cottons, prints and crisp new sari-lengths were set out enticingly on the pavement.

There were jewellers, gold and silver-smiths working in filigree in the front of their shops. High pyramids of grain were heaped in black wicker-baskets, while piles of spices brought splashes of colour to the sand on which the vendors squatted to sell their wares.

Orissa laughed when she saw a sacred bull almost too fat to walk helping himself from a food-shop as he lumbered past, infuriating the owner who was too superstitious to drive him away.

There were rickshaws and buffalo-carts moving slowly. A barber was shaving the head of a man in the gutter, and next to him a scribe, his desk on the ground, was taking a letter couching it in the elaborate, flowery words that were part of his trade.

There were numberless goats, pigeons, crows, cats, dogs, horses and people, people, people everywhere!

But soon they left Peshawar behind and the Sergeant-Major driving skilfully took them out on to the dusty, open road which was bordered by a few trees and fertile, well watered fields of grain.

Here there were no more crowds, but only a few small villages through which they must pass as they went on further and further eastwards.

Everywhere there was a profusion of birds, and Orissa remembered there were more different species of birds in this part of India than in all the rest of the country.

She saw in the distance a Sarus crane, which was the height of a man, a bearded vulture with a wing span of over eight feet and hundreds of grey-winged blackbirds, whistling thrushes and magpie-robins.

"Did you hear any news when we were in the town?" Orissa asked, letting her sari fall back from her face now there was no-one to see her.

"Only rumours, Mem-sahib," the Sergeant-Major answered, "but rumours start from truth."

"In other words, there is no smoke without fire," Orissa remarked with a smile.

"I hope Colonel-Sahib not angry if I bring Mem-sahib into danger," the Sergeant-Major said.

The way he spoke told Orissa that the idea was worrying him and she said re-assuringly:

"I promise you, Sergeant-Major, if my Uncle is angry, I will direct his wrath onto me. It was I who commanded you to escort me, and when the Colonel knows why, he will understand."

Orissa's promise seemed to re-assure the Sergeant-Major, but after they had stopped in a small village to water the horse and to buy some fresh fruit she thought he looked more anxious when they went again.

"More bad news?" she enquired. "I cannot believe that it is worse than usual."

She remembered the reports of ambushes and attacks published in the English newspapers in previous years, when the Russians had been 'sabre-rattling' in all countries adjoining the North-West Frontier.

Then in 1880, Abdurrahman Khan had been recognised as the Amir of Kabul in return for his acknowledgement of the British Raj to control his foreign relations.

It had been hoped that this would bring some measure of peace, but unfortunately such optimism had been short-lived.

They drove on until Orissa was glad to open her bag and take out the woollen cloak she had worn when she left Tilbury.

Ahead lay a dim, flat plain but beyond that, there were sunny peaks where the sun still lingered.

On the road they were now passing frontiersmen who strode by with long, lifting steps.

There was one young tribesman they

passed who walked as if he was dancing. He was singing to himself and had oil-bobbed hair with a red flower in it.

More than once camels came sailing through the dust, riding towards Peshawar like ships to port from distant seas. The camel-bells tinkled merrily and then grew fainter and fainter until again they were lost in the dust.

The camels must have come from Afghanistan, Orissa thought, right through the war zone, perhaps from Russia across the Oxus and over the snowy Hindu-Kush.

Even to think of the far-away mountains made her shiver, and the Sergeant-Major thinking she must be cold said:

"Not long now, Mem-Sahib."

"Where are we stopping?" she asked, well aware they could not reach Shuba in one day.

"In a Dak-bungalow, Mem-Sahib."

Swiftly the sun slipped down behind the distant peaks, painting for a few seconds, their faces, the *tika-gharri,* and the landscape red as blood.

Then night fell like a gossamer veil of blue over the land and a sharp wind blew from the Khyber Pass to chill Orissa's neck.

They reached the bungalow a few minutes later. It was small and sparcely furnished because such bungalows only contain the essentials. Most travellers bring all their comforts they require with them.

At the sight of the Sergeant-Major and Orissa the *Khansamah* was thrown into confusion because Dak-bungalows were supposed to be reserved for European travellers.

The Sergeant-Major however quickly brow-beat him into subservience and Orissa was taken into one of the rooms and, like magic, pillows and a quilt for the bare Charpoy were provided.

An oil lamp was set on the table in the centre room which served as a living and dining-room for all travellers who spent the night in the bungalow.

Fortunately there were no other visitors and soon there was the fragrance of wood-smoke on the night air, the smell of ghee and curds, of sesame oil and mustard which had the most pungent smell of all.

Orissa washed herself, shook the dust from her sari and brushed it from her hair.

It was amusing, she thought, to let her long dark hair hang down her back as an Indian woman would have done and not to have to bother to confine it with pins or ribbons, combs or nets.

Her bracelets, given her by the kind

Indian ladies in the train, tinkled as she moved and she liked the sound of them.

Later after she had eaten, waited on by the Sergeant-Major, she heard the soft music of a sitar playing outside and learnt that a party of Indians had arrived and camped for the night in the shelter of the Dak-bungalow.

Orissa peeped at them as they sat round the fire they had kindled of dung-cake. She had brief glimpses of their faces in the lights from the flames.

They were grey-bearded Oorayas, felt-hatted, duffle-clad hillmen from the North, and strong eagle-faced men who pulled deep at gurgling hookahs, which sounded like bull-frogs.

Orissa was tired because there is nothing more exhausting than driving through the dust and heat of India, but she almost resented having to sleep in case she should miss something exciting.

This was a wild adventure such as she had never expected to encounter.

She knew only too well how conventional a British woman's life could be in India with its round of social entertainment, where after a short while one always met the same people, heard the same conversations and listened to the same complaints and the same jokes.

This experience however was something she had not even dreamt she might ever enjoy and she knew she would remember every moment of it all her life.

Finally because she really was tired she went into the bedroom, and putting on a very English white muslin nightgown buttoned to the neck and with long sleeves that reached to her wrists, she got into bed and drew over herself the wadded cotton quilt which the *Khansamah* had provided for her.

She fell asleep almost instantly and it seemed to her that she had only just closed her eyes when there was a knock on the door and she knew it was the Sergeant-Major.

"Breakfast ready five minutes, Mem-Sahib."

It was fun to be able to dress so quickly. Orissa only had to put on the short bodice which ended but a few inches below her breasts, wrap her sari around her and slip her hennaed feet into the flat sandals.

She packed everything else into her bag but kept out her cloak, knowing that if they did not reach the Fort before dark it would certainly be necessary.

In the sitting-room the Sergeant-Major

was waiting and Orissa looked at him in surprise.

He was not wearing his uniform.

"Mem-Sahib will excuse," he apologised seeing the expression on her face. "It safer for rest of journey I not look like soldier."

"I think it is very sensible of you, Sergeant-Major," Orissa said seating herself at the table.

The Sergeant-Major went to fetch her breakfast and Orissa noticed that every time he went out of the room and came back into it, he very carefully shut the door.

It was then she realised that, if she had been the Indian woman she pretended to be, she would not be sitting at the table.

"You must remind me how to behave, Sergeant-Major," she smiled, "otherwise I shall give the game away by making mistakes."

"All right here, Mem-Sahib," the Sergeant-Major replied. "I tell the *Khansamah* you very important Indian lady — a Ranee. He think strange you have no retinue, but I explain."

"How have you explained it?" Orissa asked.

The Sergeant-Major looked embarrassed.

"I tell him lady run away from wicked Rajah to find true-love," he replied.

Orissa laughed.

"Oh, Sergeant-Major, you are a romanticist!"

She realised he did not know what she meant, and sensing he was in a hurry to get back on the road, she finished her breakfast and pulling her sari over her face climbed back into the *tika-gharri.*

Soon they were driving on towards the mountains. The snowy peaks rose high into the clouds, the sky was translucent and at this early hour of the morning the air was fresh and invigorating.

The road was bad and sometimes almost obliterated by recent rains which had flooded the rivers they passed, but their horse having rested during the night kept up an even pace.

The road twisted and turned and Orissa was certain that had they travelled as the crow flew they would have reached Shuba in half the time.

Soon there were mountains on either side of them and the land was no longer flat nor the road so dusty.

Because she had the feeling the Sergeant-Major was somewhat tense she talked to him, asking him about his family and if he liked the Army.

"Mem-Sahib, it is my life!"

Orissa knew the Sikhs were great fighting men and had been defeated by the British in 1849 only after several fierce battles. They had also been loyal during the mutiny.

They were happy men because their religion combined Islamic and Hindu beliefs and to Sikhs all men were equal before God.

But Orissa had forgotten, if she ever knew, most of their religious rites.

"We are a good people," the Sergeant-Major said, now speaking not in English but in Urdu so as to keep up their disguised roles even when they were alone.

"What rites do you have?" she asked.

"Every Sikh,' the Sergeant-Major replied, "swear to keep the five 'Ks'."

"What are they?" Orissa enquired.

"Kesh," he answered, "to wear long hair. *Kangha* — a comb in the hair. *Kachha* — a soldier's shorts. *Kara* — a steel bangle, and *Kirpan* — a sabre."

"Oh, that is not difficult to remember," Orissa smiled. "But is it not a nuisance if your hair grows very long?"

"Some of us grumble, Mem-Sahib, but when you have worn it long since child, it no more difficult for man than woman."

"And what are you forbidden to do?" Orissa enquired.

"We may not drink alcohol nor smoke,"

the Sergeant-Major replied, "and the ideal of all Sikhs is a happily married life even for our gurus."

"I have always heard from my father what magnificent fighters you are," Orissa said.

"The most sacred, the most venerable object in any Sikh family," the Sergeant-Major answered, "is the sword."

Orissa knew this was true, and she remembered when she was a child seeing Sikhs in Lahore, each of them as they walked about the streets carrying his big, sometimes clumsy sword, which had been handed down from father to son over many generations.

They drove on, stopping sometimes to give the horse a rest. By the middle of the day the sun was very hot so that Orissa was glad to get out of the *tika-gharri* and sit in the shade of a deodar tree.

Now the clouds had vanished from the distant mountains and the sky was brilliant and cloudless.

It was the end of the winter and next month there would be a steady rise in temperature day after day until the break of the rains in June.

There were still trees by the road side, deodars, junipers, and maples. There were also long valleys of sand and dunes with rough shrubs covering the surrounding hills. On the hill-tops there were only bare boulders in an untidy confusion as if thrown by a giant in some Herculean test of strength.

When they were in a valley between the hills the air was almost stifling, but then there would sometimes come a little breath of wind which was very welcome.

On and on they went until Orissa found her eyes closing sleepily.

She became unconscious of her surroundings, being only dreamily aware of the tritt-trot of the horse's hoofs and the rumble of the wheels when they encountered a more stony part of the road.

They stopped, ate and drank, and went on again. Now the travellers they passed were few and far between.

"It appears quiet enough here at any rate!" Orissa said for something to say.

"I hopes so, Mem-Sahib," the Sergeant-Major replied.

Orissa knew from the tone of his voice he was worried.

Once she thought far away in the distance she heard the sound of shots and she knew that the Sergeant-Major heard it too.

Yet when they both lifted their heads listening intently like terrier dogs, Orissa could not be certain that it had not just been a rock fall in the mountains.

On they went, and now the road was very rough and the hills rising on either side of them were more rugged than they had been before.

They drove beside a river which was flowing down from the mountains, sparkling and clear as it ran over the stones. Orissa knew that soon the heat of summer would dry it up altogether and leave only dark, muddy patches to tell of its passage.

The horse seemed untiring, despite the fact that with such heavy-going it was not an easy drive.

Perhaps it sensed that ahead of it lay food and a comfortable stable for the night, but whatever the reason for its endurance Orissa knew it had been well worth whatever price the Sergeant-Major had paid for it.

He had already explained to her that there was nothing left of the money she had handed to him.

"I am not surprised, Sergeant-Major," Orissa said, "and I am sure that I am in your debt. My Uncle will compensate you for any of your own money you may have expended on my behalf."

"Thank you, Mem-Sahib," he said with dignity.

She was well aware that he had a great

pride as had all Sikhs, and she had the feeling that if he could afford not to ask for extra money he would have done so.

"Tell me about Shuba," she begged.

She had a feeling that the emptiness of the road and the bleakness of the mountains on either side of them was somehow eerie and un-human.

"I not been there before, Mem-Sahib," the Sergeant-Major answered.

Orissa noticed that he had lowered his voice as if afraid they might be overheard.

"It is an old Fort?"

"No, Mem-Sahib, but not often in use."

That alone told Orissa that the situation was serious.

She remembered hearing in the past complaints that there were never enough troops to guard the frontier. That they were now manning extra and usually unnecessary Forts meant that the authorities were definitely anticipating trouble.

They drove on. It was getting late in the day and the sun was beginning to sink when at last the Sergeant-Major with a note of triumph in his voice exclaimed:

"Shuba!"

He pointed as he spoke and there ahead, golden against the mountains behind it,

Orissa could see the roofs and walls of a Fort.

It was built on the plan of all British forts encircled by a mud wall and standing high so that an enemy to approach it would be at the disadvantage of having a steep climb before he would reach even the outer walls.

"We have done it, Sergeant-Major!" Orissa said in triumph.

"Yes, Mem-Sahib."

"It appears quiet and peaceful," Orissa said.

She looked round as she spoke at the snowy peaks beyond the Fort and the mountains ranging away to the East and West.

"When tribesmen fight, one does not see man until he shoot," the Sergeant-Major said grimly.

Orissa remembered Major Meredith's words when he had said:

"Behind every rock and wadi of the North West Frontier, savage tribesmen lie in ambush."

They still had at least three miles to go before they could reach Shuba, and Orissa suddenly had the uncanny feeling they were being watched.

Were there savage tribesmen on either side of them, perhaps at this moment looking down the long barrels of their rifles preparing to take aim?

Now she saw the reason why the Sergeant-Major had set aside his uniform.

"Perhaps," she said aloud, "if the enemy are watching us, they will not think us worth a bullet!"

"Let us hope that so, Mem-Sahib," the Sergeant-Major agreed, his voice tense.

'I am sure I am imagining such things,' Orissa told herself.

Yet she had an unmistakable feeling of danger, almost a presentiment that they might not reach Shuba.

For the first time since they had left Peshawar the Sergeant-Major applied his whip forcibly on the back of their horse.

It hastened its pace until the fragile little *tika-gharri* swayed from side to side and the rumble of the wheels grew louder. It was almost as if they were being pursued and only speed could bring them in safety to the security of the Fort.

Orissa held on to the side of the cart so that she could keep her balance on the hard wooden seat.

'Why should I be frightened?' she asked herself. 'It looks so peaceful!'

The Fort and the mountains ahead were

192

suddenly bathed in a deeper and more glorious light.

Overhead the sky was still clear. There was not even the shimmer of the first evening star. But the valley through which they were travelling on the last lap of their journey was in shadow and only the tops of the mountains flanking them held the brilliance of the sinking sun.

'Please God, let us reach Shuba safely,' Orissa prayed in her heart.

She could not explain why she should be frightened, and yet she knew she was.

She remembered as a child she had always had a strange perception in India — she had known spiritual experiences which she could not understand and had an awareness of something beyond the commonplace.

She had always known that behind the world as she knew it there was another, and that the gods and goddesses her Ayah and the Indian servants worshipped were as real to her as to them.

Now because she was in India and because she vibrated to impulses beyond the logic of her brain, she knew irrefutably that she and the Sergeant-Major were at this moment within an inch of losing their lives.

'Keep us safe! Please . . . keep us safe!' Orissa whispered.

She was sure that the Sikh was praying to the God of his ancestors and she prayed to hers.

Still the little horse trotted on, until crossing a flat plain they reached the foot of the incline which led up to the Fort itself.

The road twisted and turned to make the climb easier for the bullocks which pulled the heavy guns, for the horses which dragged the wagons, and the soldiers who must march up on their feet after perhaps a very long journey in the heat of the plains.

They were climbing, climbing, and Orissa held her breath lest at the last moment the danger she sensed so vividly should materialise in the shape of a bullet.

Then as the horse turned for the last time and she saw ahead of her the large nail-studded gate leading into the Fort was open and two sentries were standing just inside it.

She turned her head to smile at the Sergeant-Major.

"Thank you, Sergeant-Major," she said in English. "A quick, comfortable and easy journey."

"I grateful, Mem-Sahib, we arrive without incident," the Sergeant-Major replied.

They drove in through the open gate. A soldier carrying his rifle came to the side of the *tika-gharri.*

"Who are you and what do you want?" he asked in English.

"Sergeant-Major Hari Singh reporting for duty!"

'Well, I'll be damned!" the soldier ejaculated.

Then encountering the Sergeant-Major's eyes he stepped back to salute smartly.

"Pass, Sergeant-Major."

They moved on and now Orissa saw a number of soldiers hurrying towards them.

"The Sergeant-Major! Oi don't believe it!" one of them exclaimed.

"Yer did it! Oi bet five bob t'were impossible!" another said.

A cheer went up from them all.

A Corporal came to the side of the cart.

"Colonel wishes t'see yer immediately — whoever you might be!"

"Show the way," the Sergeant-Major ordered.

"Follow me, Sergeant-Major!"

The man ran ahead and the Sergeant-Major drove after him ignoring the startled questions, the exclamations and the excitement of the soldiers clustering round the cart.

Orissa knew they were looking at her with

undisguised curiosity, but she kept her face covered.

They went through narrow streets of shops and native dwellings until they reached the strongly built fortified centre where there was both the Citadel and the Commander's residence.

Surprisingly it was a pleasant house built in English fashion with a verandah, an impressive porch and a garden.

Again they were challenged by a sentry who recognised the Sergeant-Major before he replied and came sharply to attention as they alighted.

The soldier who had led the way took the *tika-gharri* away and a soldier-servant led them across what seemed a conventional hall and opened a door.

"Sergeant-Major Singh to see you, Sir," he announced in a stentorian voice.

The oil lamp had not been lit and it was dim in the Sitting-room but Orissa saw her Uncle rise from a large desk in the centre of the room.

"Good God, Sergeant-Major!" he ejaculated, "was it you driving that *tika-gharri?* I told them to bring me the fool who was risking his life as soon as he arrived, but I hardly expected it to be you!"

Orissa moved forward.

"It was the only way I could get here, Uncle Henry!" she exclaimed.

She pushed back her sari from her head and ran towards her Uncle.

He stared at her incredulously as if she was a stranger who had taken leave of her senses.

"Uncle Henry, I am Orissa! Surely you recognise me even dressed in this?" Orissa cried. "I had to come to you! There was nothing else I could do. Step-mother turned me out into the snow and Charles sent me out to you!"

She paused and having reached her Uncle's side looked at him appealingly, half afraid of the expression on his face.

"Orissa!" Colonel Hobart said wonderingly. "It is really Orissa?"

"You do not seem very pleased to see me, Uncle Henry," Orissa exclaimed, half laughing at his astonishment, "but Charles promised to send you a telegram to announce my arrival and of course he forgot. You know what Charles's memory is like!"

Colonel Hobart put his arms around her shoulders.

"My dear child," he said in a strange voice, "I can hardly credit that you are here and that you are — safe!"

"It is entirely due to the Sergeant-Major,"

Orissa said, "and you are not to be angry with him for bringing me. I made him. There was nothing else I could do."

"Then I must thank you, Sergeant-Major," the Colonel said, "you must tell me the whole story later, when you are in uniform."

"Very good, Sir."

The Sergeant-Major saluted and moved with military precision from the room.

Orissa's eyes were still on her Uncle's face.

"You must not be cross with me, Uncle Henry," she pleaded, "but you know what Step-mama is like. She was drunk, it was snowing, and I would have frozen to death if I had not stayed the night at Charles's lodgings. I could not go on doing that as they were Army lodgings, and he would have got into trouble if he had been found out!"

"I do not know if I am standing on my head or my heels, Orissa!" Colonel Hobart said. "Do you realise we have been watching your approach from the top of the Fort and expecting to see you shot down at any moment?"

"I felt it! I felt I was in danger," Orissa said, "But nothing happened."

"By a miracle!" a deep voice interposed.

Orissa started so violently that she almost wrenched herself from her Uncle's arms.

She had not thought there was anyone else present except her Uncle. But now she saw a man rise from a chair in the shadows at the side of the room.

It was Fate — it was destiny. She could not escape and once again the man she had thought never to see again was back in her life.

"It seems incredible, does it not, Meredith?" she heard her Uncle say. "Let me introduce you to my unpredictable and quite incorrigible niece. Major Myron Meredith — Lady Orissa Fane."

Major Meredith walked towards the desk and now he stood only a few feet from Orissa looking at her.

The shock of his appearance had swept the colour from her cheeks and her eyes, circled with kohl, seemed enormous as she stared at him, the red caste-mark vivid on her forehead.

Her hands with their hennaed nails rose instinctively towards her breast as if to soothe the tumult that his sudden appearance had caused.

"Lady Orissa and I have met before, Sir," Major Meredith said slowly.

"With Charles, I suppose?" Colonel Hobart remarked. "Both my niece and my nephew are mad-caps, but I love them!"

"Thank you . . . dear Uncle Henry," Orissa said.

She found her voice with difficulty. It was impossible to meet Major Meredith's grey eyes.

"But now you are here," Colonel Hobart went on, "I am wondering what on earth I am going to do about you."

"Why?" Orissa enquired. "I will not be any trouble!"

"Trouble!" Colonel Hobart exclaimed.

Then suddenly he laughed.

"If it were not so serious, it would be extremely funny," he said. "Here we are, boxed up in this Fort, thinking ourselves besieged, and you come driving up with the Sergeant-Major and pass through what we believe to be the enemy lines completely unscathed!"

"You mean . . . that they were there . . . behind the rocks?" Orissa asked in a low voice.

"Quite a number of them!" the Colonel replied dryly.

The door opened and a soldier servant entered.

"The Officer on duty would like a word with you, Sir."

"I will go and see what he wants," the Colonel said. "Meredith, look after my niece. I expect she would like something to eat and drink after that bloodcurdling drive."

As he spoke the Colonel walked across the room towards the door.

Orissa put out her hand as if to stop him. She even took a tentative step to follow after him, and then realised there was nothing she could do but be left alone with Major Meredith.

With an effort, conscious of how strange she must look, she proudly raised her chin and said in what she hoped was a commonplace voice:

"I would like to change. Would you tell someone to show me to my room?"

"Certainly," he answered, "but you must forgive me if I am slightly bewildered, not only by your appearance here in the Fort where you will find yourself the only disruptive female influence, but also as to your identity."

"I am too tired to explain now," Orissa said evasively.

"Will you not even tell me what has happened to the inhospitable husband who was waiting for you in Bombay?"

Orissa could not help the faint smile on her lips as she replied:

"He was at least a protection from importunate gentlemen!"

"I see, Lady Orissa," Major Meredith said severely, "that you are an extremely astute and experienced liar!"

Again Orissa smiled before she replied:

"You flatter me, Major Meredith. Perhaps there will always be a career open for me on the stage!"

As she spoke she turned towards the door. Because there was nothing else he could do, the Major moved ahead and opened it for her.

He gave an order to one of the servants waiting outside in the Hall and the man led Orissa up the staircase.

She did not look back although she was well aware that Major Meredith was watching her go.

She hoped he appreciated how graceful her sari was. She had the feeling that at last she had surprised and discomfited him.

Now he would realise that his suspicions about her were entirely without foundation and that he had in fact behaved in a very reprehensible manner.

'It will teach him a sharp lesson!' Orissa told herself.

And yet she would not face the fact that deep in her heart she had been glad to see him!

CHAPTER SEVEN

The Indian bearer was unpacking Orissa's canvas hold-all in the Bed-room.

She walked across the room to look out of the window but found there was very little to see as the house was sheltered by trees and a twenty-five foot high wall.

"Mem-Sahib like bath?" the bearer enquired.

"Yes, please," Orissa answered.

She thought how wonderful it would be to feel really clean after the dust she had encountered on the journey.

She could not undress until the big cans of hot and cold water had been brought into a small room adjoining hers where there was a large tin bath which, she knew, Officers of Regiments always used when in India.

This took a little time and she sat down in her room thinking, although she tried not to, of Major Meredith and what a shock it had been to encounter him when she had least expected it.

It was not easy to understand how he had reached the Fort before she had.

He must obviously have taken the fast, morning train from Bombay to Delhi and would therefore have caught an earlier train to Peshawar than she had been able to do.

But having reached Peshawar, how then could he have made his way to the Fort if, as her Uncle said, they were under siege and they had expected her and the Sergeant-Major to be shot down before they reached safety?

It all seemed very incomprehensible to Orissa and she hoped her Uncle would explain everything to her later.

The bearer announced that her bath was ready, so she slipped off her sari and stepped into the warm water delighted to be able to wash not only the travel marks but also the henna from her hands and feet.

It was not easy, however, to remove the henna on her nails and she thought that tomorrow she would ask if there was anything the Indian women used that would clean it away completely.

When she had bathed she poured some water into a basin and washed her hair.

She was horrified at the amount of dust it had collected, and when she had dried it

the blue lights were back in its shining darkness and it was no longer the smudgy grey
it had become from the clinging dust.

She went into the Bed-room, putting on a
muslin wrapper, and sat in front of the
dressing-table to finish drying her hair and
then to brush it.

She was looking at her reflection in the
mirror and thinking that perhaps she was
more attractive with kohl round her eyes,
when suddenly there was a sharp exchange
of gun-fire, a staccato burst followed by
another and yet another so rapid that the
effect was deafening.

For a moment Orissa sat motionless, too
startled to move. Then there was a knock
on the door, and without waiting for her
reply her Uncle entered the room.

"What is it? What is happening?" Orissa
asked.

"I was afraid you might be frightened," he
replied, "so I came to tell you that this
always occurs as soon as it is dark."

"Are the tribesmen attacking us?" Orissa
questioned.

"They are showing us they are there!" he
said, "but they have not yet attempted to
storm the Fort."

At that moment there was the heavy
"boom" of an artillery gun followed by

several more salvos and Colonel Hobart could not speak until the sound of them died away.

"Explain . . . please explain what is happening?" Orissa begged.

She was no longer frightened; her voice was quite steady and she thought that her Uncle looked at her with approval.

"I heard on board ship that the Army was expecting trouble," she went on.

"We are not only expecting it, we have got it!" Colonel Hobart said grimly.

"From whom?" Orissa asked knowing the answer.

"The Russians of course," the Colonel replied. "They have made, as you know, a great many conquests over the past years: — Bokhara, Khiva and Kokland, now they are harassing Afghanistan."

"But why?" Orissa asked.

"Because they see a chance to threaten Britain through the 'back door' of her Indian Empire," Colonel Hobart answered.

"But surely we can defend India?" Orissa asked.

"We have only thirty soldiers for each mile of the Frontier," Colonel Hobart answered, "recent reports have made it clear that every man that can be spared from duty in other parts of India must be here."

"The Sergeant-Major told me that this Fort is not usually manned."

"It has always had a token force to guard it," Colonel Hobart replied, "but we rely on the larger Forts like Quelta to show our strength."

"And who is firing at us at the moment?" Orissa enquired.

"Tribesmen led by Russians who have infiltrated across the border and are doing their best, so Meredith thinks, to stir up a Holy war."

"Like what has been happening in the Sudan?" Orissa remarked.

"Exactly!" Colonel Hobart agreed. "And at the moment they are making it very uncomfortable for the British defences — especially ourselves."

He paused and then he said:

"As you very probably know our confrontation with Russia is known as the 'Great Game', but for the moment, as far as we are personally concerned, it is more serious than a game."

"Are we really besieged?" Orissa asked.

"I understand," Colonel Hobart said slowly, "that there are tribesmen in their thousands encamped all around us in the mountains, whilst my fighting force here in Shuba, both British and native, amounts to barely eight hundred!"

There was a violent burst of firing which seemed almost to shake the room.

Orissa was silent until it died down a little, and then she said:

"Have they . . . killed many . . . of our soldiers?"

"A number of civilians who live in the Fort have been killed," Colonel Hobart answered. "Half a dozen of our men were wounded yesterday, two mortally. We can only hope we have inflicted some casualties upon the enemy."

He drew nearer to her as he spoke and put his hand on her shoulder.

"I want you to know the truth, Orissa, but I have no wish to frighten you," he said. "You have certainly set me a problem by coming here at this moment, but let us enjoy being together. For the moment I can say no more about our position until perhaps tomorrow or the next day."

"How will you know more then?" Orissa asked curiously.

But it seemed as if her Uncle had not heard, for he was already moving towards the door.

"Dinner will be ready in ten minutes," he said as he left.

Orissa finished dressing quickly, putting

on the only evening gown she had brought with her which the native bearer had pressed carefully while she was having her bath.

When she was ready she thought if anyone looked at her now, they would not suppose for a moment she had just taken part in a hair-raising adventure.

It was only as she turned to walk downstairs that she realised she was wearing the peacock-blue gown she had worn the night on board ship when Major Meredith had kissed her!

She only hoped that he would not think it indicated she had forgiven him for his indiscretion.

Then she felt the blood rise to her face as she thought perhaps he might take it as an invitation to repeat such audacity.

But with a little shrug of her shoulders she decided it did not matter what he thought — it was all she had to wear, and as she would have to wear it night after night he would soon realise that her wardrobe was limited.

Colonel Hobart was waiting for her in the Drawing-room which looked very English with glazed-chintz curtains, comfortable sofas and small tables on which reposed vases of flowers.

He was wearing the Mess-kit of the Royal

Chilterns with the short, red, blue lapelled jacket which made him and the other officers awaiting Orissa's arrival look exceedingly smart.

There was a Major, a Captain and two Subalterns dining with them and Orissa soon realised that in their eyes she was a heroine.

"It was incredibly brave of you!" the Major ejaculated.

And there was no mistaking the admiration in the Subalterns' expressions.

"Do tell us all about it from the very beginning," the Captain begged. "Was it your idea or the Sergeant-Major's that you should travel with him disguised as an Indian woman?"

The dinner was served with much ceremony and was delicious. Orissa found herself enjoying the conventional English dishes, although she really preferred the hot curries which she had found so delectable on the journey.

"It is a pity we could not have offered you some young venison for dinner," the Major said conversationally, "but unfortunately our shooting has been rather restricted since we have been here!"

He laughed as he spoke, and then explained to Orissa how many different spe-

cies of animals could be found in the mountains.

Orissa was interested, but at the same time
she could not help finding herself wondering all through dinner where Major
Meredith could be and why he was not
present.

She supposed that he preferred to dine in
the Officers' Mess rather than with her
Uncle.

At the same time she could not help feeling that seeing how few troops there were
in the Fort, the Mess must be somewhat
depleted of officers as there were so many
at dinner with them.

She however said nothing, but one obser-
vation did not escape her.

One of the Subalterns said to her Uncle:

"Any news, Sir, of what numbers the
enemy have reached by now?"

"None, I am afraid," the Colonel replied.

"Well, I expect Major Meredith will be
able to tell us the worst!" the Subaltern said
with some complacency.

He suddenly caught a quick, hard look
from his Colonel's eyes and realised he had
made a mistake. The colour rose in his face
and he lapsed into silence.

It then appeared as if everyone else at the
table started to talk as if in an attempt to

cover up his slip. Orissa decided it was because the remark had been made when the servants were in the room.

But whatever the reason it was obvious that Major Meredith's name was *'taboo'* and he was not mentioned again during the whole meal.

The firing died away after about an hour of sharp exchanges, and now there was only a silence which Orissa thought was perhaps more uneasy than to hear the actual report of the guns.

When dinner was over they all moved into the Drawing-room, because as the Colonel said, the exceptional circumstances of Orissa being with them made it an excuse not to neglect her while they drank their Port.

They therefore sat around doing their best to be entertaining, and because the evening was chilly, as she had discovered on her journey, there was a cheerful fire in the grate.

It was not until the officers had left and Orissa and her Uncle were alone that she had the chance to talk about her father and Step-mother, and tell him how intolerable her life had become at home.

"I had no idea that things were so bad," Colonel Hobart said. "I blame myself for not suggesting sooner that you should come out to India and be with me."

"You were not to know how much Papa has deteriorated," Orissa said excusingly, "and I did not like to write and tell you."

"I ought to have guessed," Colonel Hobart said, "but I knew how difficult things were on the Frontier, and that if there was to be any fighting the Chilterns would be in the thick of it."

He smiled.

"Quite frankly I did not think it was the place for a young girl, but you have shown me I was wrong!"

"Then you are not angry with me for coming here?" Orissa asked.

"I do see that it was the only thing you could have done in the circumstances," her Uncle answered. "I loved your mother very deeply, Orissa. She was not only my sister, but we were always very close companions from the time we were children. I pledged myself to do everything I could both for you and Charles."

"You could not be expected to saddle yourself with a child," Orissa said, knowing that he was distressed by what she had told him. "But as long as I can stay with you now, then that will be more wonderful than I can possibly express."

"Shuba is hardly the place I would have chosen for us to set up house together," the Colonel said, with a faint smile. "Quite frankly, Orissa, I am worried that you have inadvertently walked into such a dangerous situation."

"Is it really so dangerous?"

"I am trying to be optimistic about it," the Colonel answered, "but perhaps I shall be able to answer that question more competently tomorrow."

"How does it concern Major Meredith?"

Orissa had hesitated before she had asked the question, but she had known that she must try to find out the truth.

Her Uncle rose to his feet to stand with his back to the fire in the inevitable position of an Englishman when he is thinking before he said:

"What do you know about Myron Meredith?"

"I know very little about him," Orissa replied. "Charles in fact warned me against him. He said he was always 'snooping' around, making trouble."

Her Uncle smiled a little wryly.

"I think if Charles were honest," he said, "he would admit that Meredith saved him from making a fool of himself. We both know Charles can be carried away very easily by a pretty face!"

Orissa laughed.

"That is true! Charles's love affairs are too numerous for anyone to keep count! But what have they to do with Major Meredith?"

Colonel Hobart did not answer.

He was frowning slightly and Orissa was well aware he was considering how much he should tell her and how much he should keep back.

"Charles told me," she went on as her Uncle did not speak, "that Major Meredith was really responsible for Gerald Dewar's shooting himself!"

"That is not true!" Colonel Hobart retorted sharply, "and Charles had no right to say such a thing."

"He said he was quite certain that Gerald would never have taken his life ordinarily. He was not that sort of man."

"No, he was not!" Colonel Hobart agreed. "But as you have heard so much, you had better hear the rest, although you must promise me, Orissa, that anything I tell you will not go beyond these four walls."

"No, of course not, Uncle Henry."

"Gerald Dewar became infatuated with a woman he met at Simba. He was so involved that he passed information to her that affected the security of our troops."

"How could he have done such a thing?" Orissa asked.

"To put it in plain English — she was a Russian spy!" the Colonel replied. "She got young Dewar into her clutches so that he was indiscreet to the point of being a traitor."

"I cannot believe it!" Orissa exclaimed. "He was Charles's friend!"

"Yes, I know that," the Colonel answered, "and it worried me a great deal."

"The only evidence you have of . . . this came from . . . Major Meredith?" Orissa asked.

"The evidence we had of Dewar's indiscretions — to call it by a more polite name than treachery —" the Colonel replied, "was when a Company of our men led by one of our best young officers was ambushed and annihiliated on the way to the Frontier."

"Oh no!" Orissa's exclamation seemed to ring out through the room.

"Unfortunately it is true," the Colonel said. "It meant of course a Court Martial for Dewar, dishonour to the Regiment, and a scandal which could not help being extremely bad for the morale of the troops."

Orissa said nothing.

She could hardly believe what her Uncle

was telling her and yet she knew it must be the truth.

"There was nothing else that Dewar could do," he said quietly, "but behave like a gentleman."

Orissa awoke to find the sun streaming in through her window and to know with a lilt in her heart that even if she were in a besieged Fort, she was with someone who loved her, and she was in India!

She rang for the bearer who brought her early morning tea and she went downstairs to breakfast with her Uncle on eggs and bacon, toast and marmalade.

"I hope you will find something with which to occupy your time, Orissa," the Colonel said, "but I am afraid I must restrict you to the house and garden. I do not wish you to be seen in the town. Your arrival has caused enough curiosity as it is."

Orissa was disappointed, but when she glanced out of the window she saw on the verandah there were a number of vendors squatting down with their goods for sale and she turned to smile at her Uncle with a twinkle in her eyes.

"I will certainly do as you say, Uncle Henry," she said, "if you will give me some money!"

"Are you trying to blackmail me?" Colonel Hobart asked.

"I am afraid I am likely to prove a very expensive guest," Orissa answered.

"But a very attractive one," he said, "so my bank balance is at your disposal. Here for the moment are enough rupees to enable some of those rascals outside to retire for life!"

Orissa took the rupees he gave her and reached up to kiss his cheek.

"It will be so wonderful to have some pretty clothes again," she said. "Step-Mama grudged every penny Papa gave me and I really have looked like a tattered Cinderella for years."

"If we ever get out of this mess, I will buy you the most beautiful gowns that Lahore, Delhi, or Madras can provide," her Uncle promised.

Then he hurried away to leave Orissa to her bargaining.

She spent an entrancing morning fingering the silks, embroidered gauzes and brilliantly coloured muslins that the vendors displayed for her.

She was astonished to find such beautiful materials in such a small, out-of-the-way place as Shuba, but she realised that to the Indians where there were soldiers there was always money.

A few questions elicited the fact that one man had brought his goods from Peshawar a month ago. And besides the things which came from that city there were exquisite products of Kashmir.

There were delicate chain-stitched carpets, walnut wood carved and polished to a satin finish. This, Orissa learnt, was done with sandal-wood powder rubbed in with an agate stone.

There was Kashmir wool — Paschmina, spun from goats-beard hair and silks which had more subtle colours than those from any other part of India.

"Look, Mem-Sahib," the Indian said beguilingly, "Kashmiri embroidered shawl, can pull through ring, so light, so delicate!"

Orissa smiled, but it was true. She had never seen such soft and delicate shawls or such beautiful little objects made of papier-mâché and painted with gold-leaf.

She tried to spend her Uncle's money sparingly, but she found it hard to resist a bottle of pure Jasmin oil, filigree earrings that she had seen the native craftsmen making when she had passed through Peshawar and small semi-precious stones dug from the mountains, cornelians, amethysts and lapis-lazuli.

She was so intent on her purchases and so fascinated by the tales of the men who sold them to her that it was time for *tiffin* before she realised that the morning had passed, and she had not yet finally decided on all she would buy.

The vendors were quite happy to remain on the verandah and even to wait after luncheon when Orissa in traditional Indian fashion took a siesta.

She did not feel tired having slept well the night before, but she knew that the household would expect it and she therefore went upstairs to lie on her bed.

It seemed impossible to believe that they were really besieged in the Fort, and yet just before dawn the firing had broken out again to awaken her with a start.

"They're at it morning and night, regular as clock-work!" her Uncle's Cockney soldier-servant told her cheerily.

"It is certainly very noisy," Orissa admitted.

"That's what they like," the Soldier answered, "noise — and th' chance to cut some'un to pieces with their long knives."

Orissa shuddered.

It was easy to forget temporarily the danger they were in, and then she told herself that her Uncle must be expecting reinforcements.

He did not come back to luncheon but he arrived in the house at about four o'clock and Orissa saw the servants carrying in a very good imitation of an English tea.

There was fruit cake, sandwiches and small fairy-cakes such as she had enjoyed as a child, tea hot and strong, while only the milk was strange having come from a goat not a cow.

"I expected you back to luncheon," Orissa said.

"I should have sent a bearer to make my excuses," her Uncle said. "We were having a Council of War."

"Will you tell me what has been happening?" Orissa asked.

"I do not wish to depress you," Colonel Hobart replied.

"I would much rather know the truth."

"I can understand that! The real trouble is that the tribesmen have been clever enough to cut all our communications with Headquarters."

"So you cannot get a message to Peshawar to say that you are besieged!" Orissa exclaimed.

"Exactly!" her Uncle agreed.

"Would it not be possible to send a messenger?"

"We have already tried that," her Uncle answered. "Two men set out — one three nights ago and the next the following night."

He paused and Orissa looked at him expectantly.

"Their heads were tossed over the wall the next morning."

Orissa drew in her breath.

"We got through . . . the Sergeant-Major and I," she said. "How did that happen?"

"Meredith believes," her Uncle said, "that it was not just chance or luck, but because the tribesmen wished to lull us into a sense of false security. They hoped perhaps we might send out further messengers and if one did get through he would report that access to the Fort was not impossible because two people had arrived unscathed."

Orissa looked at her Uncle wonderingly and then she said slowly:

"You mean that any Force coming to . . . relieve you would . . . imagine they could get through, and then . . ."

"They would be ambushed!" Colonel Hobart completed. "It is impossible to reach the Fort except by the road and for a troop of soldiers to come along the valley at this moment would be sheer murder!"

Orissa heard the pain in his voice and saw the anxiety in his eyes.

"Then what can you do?" she asked.

"That is what I am waiting to find out," Colonel Hobart replied.

And Orissa knew, though he did not say so, that somehow the answer was connected with Major Meredith.

She found herself wondering late that night what possible solution Major Meredith could find to such a problem unless he could fly away from the Fort like a bird, or burrow under ground like a mole.

He or anyone else leaving the Fort would be at the mercy of the enemy just as any relieving Force could be shot down from both sides of the road.

She fell asleep trying to solve the problem and although she spent part of the day with the vendors of the beautiful things on the verandah, and several hours starting to make a new gown, her thoughts would not keep away from Major Meredith.

She came down to dinner that evening scented with Jasmin but with the noise of rifle fire ringing in her ears and walked into the Drawing-Room to find him alone with her Uncle.

"Here you are, Orissa!" Colonel Hobart exclaimed, "I was just about to send for you. I knew you would be glad to know that Major Meredith has returned safely."

223

"Good-evening," Orissa said cooly as if they were meeting in a London Drawing-room.

The Major bowed and she had the feeling it was slightly ironic.

He was dressed for dinner not in the colourful Mess-kit that was worn by the Bengal Lancers, but of the Royal Chilterns. Orissa thought it did not fit very well and wondered if he had borrowed it.

She also thought he was slightly thinner than when she had last seen him. The cheek-bones in his brown face seemed more pronounced and his sun-tan darker than it had been before. Then she told herself she was just imagining things.

Anyway it was difficult to tell in the soft light of the oil-lamps.

They sat down three to dinner and she noticed that Major Meredith ate quickly and appeared to be very hungry.

Orissa on the contrary found lack of air and exercise had taken away her appetite — or could it be attributed to the fact that the man she had been thinking about and who was becoming more and more of a mystery was present?

She longed to ask him questions.

Where had he been in the Fort? Why had she not seen him since the night she arrived?

But she knew it was impossible to say anything while the servants were in the room.

Finally they retired to the Drawing-Room, but her Uncle did not bring a glass of port with him, nor did Major Meredith.

Orissa noticed that the Major shut the door very firmly as he came last into the room. Then he walked towards the fireplace and Orissa knew before either he or her Uncle spoke that they were about to say something momentous.

There was something in their manner — something tense about them both — and she looked up at them from the sofa on which she was sitting, her eyes very large in her small face.

"What is it?" she asked.

"Meredith has brought me bad news," Colonel Hobart replied. "There are so many tribesmen encamped in the mountains that we can expect an assault at any moment."

Orissa said nothing. Her eyes were on her Uncle's face as he went on:

"Although the authorities may have realised our communications are cut, there is no reason to think they will be alarmed. Telegraph wires are continually being blown down or swept away by avalanches in this part of the world, and they would expect if we were in danger we would send a message by some other means."

"But you have been unable to do so," Orissa murmured.

"Meredith therefore thinks," her Uncle went on, "the only possible chance of our communicating with the British at Peshawar is for him to reach them and explain the situation."

Orissa was still for a moment before she asked:

"But why should he be more successful than anyone else? You told me this morning that two men have already been killed trying to take messages from the Fort."

"Meredith has his own methods of getting in and out of this place," Colonel Hobart answered.

"You mean . . . that was where you were . . . last night?" Orissa asked speaking directly to Major Meredith.

He slightly inclined his head but did not reply.

"What Meredith has done," her Uncle went on, "is to bribe one of the enemy to go to Peshawar. There is a chance — but it is a slim one — that he will be successful. It was in fact a wild risk for Major Meredith to take which might have resulted in his being exposed and killed on the spot."

There was a note in the Colonel's voice which told Orissa that he had already spoken sharply to Major Meredith for endangering his life in such a manner, but now her Uncle continued:

"At the same time, Major Meredith now thinks that he should go himself to ensure that if the man does get through, then reinforcements will in fact come to save us from what, if the enemy strike, might be total annihilation."

"This . . . cannot be . . . true!" Orissa said almost in a whisper.

"We have to face facts, my dear," her Uncle answered.

"Yes, of course," Orissa said striving to keep the horror out of her voice.

At the same time she could not help wondering why her Uncle was telling her all this. Then he said:

"Major Meredith has persuaded me that his plan is the only possibility of saving the men who are under my command and prevent the Fort from falling into enemy hands."

The Colonel's lips tightened.

"That would not be an overwhelming military disaster, but it would mean a great deal of loss of face as far as the British are concerned and undoubtedly encourage the tribesmen to attempt other assaults."

"I can see that," Orissa said.

"We shall therefore endeavour to hold out at all costs," the Colonel went on. "That goes without saying and Major Meredith leaves tonight."

Orissa's eyes went towards the Major.

Then her Uncle said quietly:

"You will go with him."

For a moment Orissa felt she could not have heard aright.

"Did you say . . . I would go with . . . him?"

In reply the Colonel sat down beside her on the sofa and took her hand in his.

"My dear, I have had a terrible choice to make in this matter. First to let you stay here and take a chance that the reinforcements will arrive in time, or else to believe Major Meredith when he tells me that if anyone can take you to safety it will be he."

"But I would rather stay with you," Orissa said quickly.

She felt as she spoke a stab of horror, not only at encountering the unknown danger, but of going away alone with Major Meredith.

"I would like to keep you here," Colonel Hobart replied, "but a battle taking place against such enormous odds will not be a sight for any woman's eyes, and besides . . ."

He hesitated and was obviously searching for the right words.

"What your Uncle is trying to say to you," Major Meredith interposed, "is that in the event of the Fort being overrun someone will have to shoot you!"

Orissa went very pale but she did not protest. She knew that after the Mutiny no Englishman would leave a woman to the mercy of natives inflamed by blood.

"I . . . understand," she said in a low voice.

Her Uncle rose to his feet.

"I knew that I could rely on you, Orissa," he said. "You have been brought up in the shadow of the Regiment, and you are behaving as I should expect you to behave in such circumstances."

Orissa smiled at his praise. Then she said:

"But how can I go with the Major? What should I wear? Surely I will need a disguise?"

"Of course," Major Meredith said, "but it is important, you understand, that no-one even in this household should see you leave or learn how you are disguised."

"Yes, I can see that."

"Will you therefore go upstairs at once, and tell your bearer you are going to bed early and do not wish to be disturbed in the morning. Later the Colonel will make what excuses are necessary."

Orissa rose to her feet.

"What do I do then?"

"You wait until your bearer has gone to the servants' quarters and then you come downstairs. Do not come into this room, but go to your Uncle's Study which looks onto the back of the house. There will be no servants in the Hall. They will have been sent on various errands."

"I will do as you say."

"You can of course bring nothing with you," Major Meredith said, "and to save the trouble of taking your clothes upstairs after you have changed I suggest you put on the sari you were wearing when you arrived."

"I will do that."

Orissa turned as she spoke and walked towards the door.

There really seemed nothing else to say.

She did exactly as she had been told. She went to her bedroom, rang for the bearer, told him she did not wish to be disturbed, and after he had left her, put on her sari and went quickly down the stairs.

There was, as Major Meredith had promised, no-one in the Hall and she reached her Uncle's Study at the back of the house without being seen.

The Major was waiting for her and he was alone.

"We must move as quickly as possible," he said, "so will you change into these clothes?"

As he spoke he pointed to what at first appeared to be a bundle of rags. Then Orissa realised they were the somewhat tattered garments of a boy.

"You expect me to wear . . . those?" Orissa asked in a tone of horror.

A smile twisted Major Meredith's lips for a moment as he said:

"You do not suppose you would get far through the enemy lines looking as you look now. Many of the men out there have not seen a woman for some months."

The intimation in his words made Orissa blush, then she said angrily:

"There must be some better disguise which does not show my legs."

"This is not the moment for simpering, girlish modesty," he said scathingly.

His words made Orissa even more angry.

"I can see you are determined to make our journey as unpleasant as possible!"

"You should not have come here at all, and it will not be easy to get you away."

"You are really putting yourself out on my account, are you not?" Orissa asked sarcastically. "I have no desire to accompany you, Major Meredith. It would be far easier, I am sure, to stay here and fight."

If she meant to annoy him, she succeeded.

"I can assure you, Lady Orissa," he replied in an icy tone, "I also would much rather stay here and fight; and if you really think I wish to encumber myself with a whining, complaining female, you are very much mistaken!"

If he had slapped her in the face Orissa could not have been more incensed.

She drew herself up to answer him fiercely but at that moment her Uncle came into the room.

"You should hurry," he said in an anxious tone. "The further away from the Fort you are by dawn, the safer it will be."

"I am well aware of that, Sir," Major Meredith answered. "Perhaps you would persuade your niece to change into these garments I have provided for her."

"Of course," Colonel Hobart agreed. "Hurry, Orissa, we will wait outside."

He went from the Study and Major Meredith followed him.

Orissa slipped off her sari and with some distaste put on the shapeless garments which were worn by Mohammedans. She was hardly decent before the Major knocked at the door and without waiting for an answer came in.

Orissa saw him glance at her bare legs and blushed.

Then he knelt down in front of her and proceeded to put on her feet a pair of her strongest slippers and still without speaking, he took some strips of coarse woollen material and wrapped them round her legs as the hillmen do in the cold weather, and criss-crossed them with strong strings of cotton, to hold them in place above the knee.

Colonel Hobart came into the room just as the Major had finished.

"That will certainly keep her warmer," he said approvingly.

Orissa had not loosened her hair when she changed from her evening gown into the sari, and now the Major taking a faded length of material which had once been pink but now only showed patches of its original colour, twisted it competently around her head as a turban.

While he did this, the Colonel brought from a side table a saucer in which there was some pale brown liquid.

"I shall have to stain your skin, Lady Orissa," Major Meredith said. "But only slightly; many Pathans are pale."

It was the first time he had spoken since they had raged at each other and she felt that his voice still held a note of anger.

"Will it wash off?" the Colonel asked.

"It comes off fairly easily with soap and water," Major Meredith replied curtly, "but it will not be moved by rain."

He picked up a sponge.

"Shut your eyes," he commanded.

Orissa felt him sponge her face all over and then her neck and taking her hands one after the other he continued with his work until she saw that her skin was now a soft, golden brown.

"I will just change into my own clothes, Sir," he said to Colonel Hobart.

He went from the room and her Uncle brought Orissa a small glass of wine from a side-table.

"This will fortify you on your journey, my dear," he said, "and I want to say how proud I am of you."

Orissa felt the tears come into her eyes.

"You will be all right, Uncle Henry?" she asked.

"We can only put our trust in God," Colonel Hobart replied, "and I promise you if anyone can save us it will be Major Meredith. I have implicit faith in him."

Orissa gave a little sigh.

She could not tell her Uncle how annoyed she was with the Major at that particular moment.

The Colonel put the glass into her hand and said:

"I also want you to take these."

She saw that he was offering her four small, white pills.

"What are those?" she asked.

"Two are for protection against malaria," the Colonel answered. "The other two against dysentery."

Orissa flushed.

She knew how embarrassing it would be on the trip that she was about to take if she encountered any sort of illness, let alone those that her Uncle had just mentioned.

She took the four pills from him.

"Take them with the wine," he said. "It will help them dissolve."

Obediently she put the pills onto her tongue and thinking they had a somewhat unpleasant taste drank down the whole glass of wine as her Uncle had suggested.

As she drank it she thought it was very unlike the wine which had been served at dinner.

"Uncle Henry . . ." she began and felt a sudden strange numb feeling in her head.

It was almost like a headache and yet

more intense. Then even as she thought about it . . . she found it difficult to think . . .

She was sinking . . . sinking away and although she fought frantically against the terrifying feeling of paralysis which was invading her body and making it inanimate . . . she finally lost consciousness . . .

CHAPTER EIGHT

Orissa felt her head was splitting open and her eyes were so heavy that they seemed to sink like stones into her face.

Her mouth was dry and waves of deep, unpleasant sleep seemed to keep drifting over her like shifting water.

She made an inarticulate murmur and a voice said:

"Drink this!"

She wanted to refuse, wanted to slip away into oblivion where she would not be conscious of the pain in her head. But she found herself sipping water which was cool and refreshing in her mouth.

"A little more," the voice came again.

Now she knew who spoke and with an effort tried to raise her heavy eye-lids.

She did so and gave a cry of horror.

"It is all right," Major Meredith said.

She could hardly believe the long haired and strangely marked face belonged to him, but there was no mistaking his voice.

He made her drink again by forcing the cup which held the water against her lips until, as she felt the pain of her head receding a little, she managed to murmur:

"Where am . . . I?"

He laid her back gently on what she now realised was soft sand.

"We are about seven miles west of Shuba," he answered.

Orissa was silent, trying to remember what had happened last night.

She could hear her Uncle's voice telling her to drink the glass of wine and swallow the pills.

"You . . . drugged . . . me!" she murmured.

She meant her voice to sound aggressive, but it only sounded weak and distant.

With what was almost a superhuman effort she raised herself a little and found that she was in a shallow cave.

Outside there was sunshine, brilliantly golden and now she could feel waves of heat coming in towards her.

It took her a moment to focus her eyes in the light and to look at Major Meredith.

He was sitting cross-legged on the ground beside her and for a moment she had a sudden tremor of fear that she had been deceived and it was not he but the Fakir he was impersonating.

He had long, dark, tangled hair falling to his shoulders, and round his head was the twisted cloth which just revealed the crimson caste-mark on his forehead.

He was naked to the waist, his chest was smeared with ash and slashed with streaks of ochre paint beneath the traditional bead-necklace which he wore.

His loins were girt about with a loin cloth tied in the intricate devices of a Saddhu's cincture, and she saw lying on the ground beside him a thick, woollen cloak such as the Northern Fakirs often wear when travelling in the hills.

He saw the astonishment in her face and smiled.

"India is full of Holy men," he said, "stamping, shouting and proclaiming different faiths, shaken with the force of their own zeal! All command respect from friend or foe."

"So we . . . came through the . . . enemy lines," Orissa said.

As she spoke she caught sight of her legs and gave a little cry. They were covered with bandages deeply stained with blood.

"They are only theatrical props," Major Meredith explained. "Your presumed death was my excuse for cursing the British by every god in the Asiatic Calendar. I only hope they are not effective."

He bent forward as he spoke to unwrap the stained bandages from Orissa's legs and making them into a bundle, threw them away into a corner of the cave.

"There was . . . no need for . . . you to . . . drug me," Orissa said resentfully.

"On the contrary," Major Meredith retorted, "you had to look dead, very dead, and I do not believe that even you with your capacity for acting would not have flinched at some of the sights I saw last night."

She ignored the innuendo about her acting.

"You carried me all this way?" she asked.

"About seven miles over stony ground," Major Meredith answered, "and you weigh at least a ton! It was a fearsome task!"

Orissa felt words of protest rising to her lips and then she said shrewdly:

"I have the suspicion, Major Meredith, that you are deliberately . . . provoking me as you did . . . last night."

He gave a short laugh.

"You are too perceptive. I find that people usually do what you want to do far quicker if they are needled emotionally."

Orissa put her hand to her forehead.

She was about to say that her head felt as

if it was splitting open and she was indeed angry that he should not have trusted her. Then she remembered what he had said about "snivelling, complaining women".

She could not give him the satisfaction of knowing he was right in that, if nothing else.

Carefully, because it hurt her head to move, she sat up and Major Meredith unwrapped a piece of paper in which reposed some chapattis.

"Eat. It will make you feel better," he said.

Orissa was about to refuse and then she saw the commonsense of his suggestion.

She took a small piece of chapatti and forced herself to take a bite out of it.

"What did you . . . give me?" she asked and he knew she was not referring to the food.

"A devil's draught which knocks a man out instantly, and opium."

"I thought opium gave one pleasant dreams."

"Not if you take too much of it!" he answered briefly.

"Well, I suppose I must suffer in a good cause. Are we safe here?"

She tried to speak lightly but he answered her in all seriousness:

"We have had to make a detour to avoid arousing suspicion amongst the tribes encamped along the side of the road. It means of course more miles to travel and it will take a longer time than if we could have gone straight to Peshawar."

"Do you want to move on now?" Orissa asked wondering if she was capable of walking.

"We move only at night," Major Meredith explained. "Tribesmen have eyes like hawks — they also have sentries. Fortunately these hills are full of caves as I have found before."

"Do you always go disguised as a Fakir?" Orissa enquired.

"I have quite a reputation along the Frontier," he said with a twist of his lips. "If I die, it is far more likely to be from a British bullet which kills me inadvertantly than one from the enemy."

Orissa gave a little sigh, then she said:

"If there is nothing you wish me to do at this moment, can I go to sleep?"

"I think it an extremely sensible idea," Major Meredith replied, "and it is what I intend to do myself."

He crawled as he spoke to the mouth of the cave and looked out warily keeping well in the shade. Then he came back and settled himself about a foot away from Orissa.

"Sleep well," he said, a mocking note in his voice. "I will wake you in plenty of time before we need to start on our journey South."

Orissa lay down and shut her eyes.

Then almost as if she could not help herself she asked:

"Was I really very . . . heavy?"

She heard Major Meredith chuckle.

"No heavier than the dead boy you were supposed to be."

She felt annoyed because he had not flattered her as any other man would have done.

She slept through most of the day, and when she finally awoke as the sun was sinking it was to find that the effects of the drug had worn off and her brain felt clear and alert once again.

She did not refuse the chapatti which Major Meredith gave her and she had a drink of the water from the water bottle. She knew without asking it was something he did not bother to carry when he was alone.

She remembered how hungry he had seemed at dinner the night before and she was certain on his usual sorties he either went hungry or relied on offerings from 'the faithful' who believed in his powers.

Outside, below the cave where they were hiding, there was a country of great peaks and deep valleys. The intense sunshine of which Orissa had felt the warmth all day was now lessening as the shadows lengthened to turn the tops of the mountains and rocks gold, pink and mauve in a last burst of glory.

The air was still, clear and sparkling, but Orissa had a feeling it would soon turn cold and they would feel the wind blowing off the snows.

"How can you bear to wear so little clothing?" she asked curiously.

She was aware that after the first glance she had hardly looked at Major Meredith, embarrassed at seeing a white man so naked.

"I have hardened my body over the years," he replied. "It is you I am worried about."

"I shall be warm enough."

"I hope so," he answered, "but I did steal for you some protection from the cold."

He drew from under his own cloak as he spoke one of the hillmen's woollen blankets. It was nothing more or less than a large square of wool with a hole in the centre for the head.

"It may not be very clean," he warned, "but at least it will keep out the worst of the wind."

Orissa found this was true when as soon

as darkness fell they left the cave and started to walk along an extremely narrow and stony track which could barely be traversed even in single file.

At first she found it almost impossible to see anything but Major Meredith's body moving in front of her, his head silhouetted against the sky.

Then as the stars came out growing brighter every moment and her eyes grew accustomed to the dark, she was able to distinguish things more clearly but she had little time to think of anything but keeping up with him.

He walked with the easy stride of an athlete which was both rhythmic and graceful. Although his feet were bare he seemed not to mind the roughness of the path or that sometimes they had to pass through spiky undergrowth which Orissa felt painful even through the wrappings on her legs.

After they had walked for an hour she was aware that she was already beginning to flag a little, but she told herself that even if she died in the attempt she would not complain or ask him to go slower.

She knew also without his saying so that they were still too near to the tribesmen encamped around the Fort for it to be anything but risky to be moving at all, and she half-expected to hear the sudden report of a gun and the whistle of a bullet as it went past them.

On and on they went and only when they had been walking for over two hours did Major Meredith ask if she would like to rest.

He must have heard her stumble several times in the last few minutes, she thought, and while she was longing and aching to sit down if only for a few seconds, she managed to reply with a note almost of indifference in her voice:

"That would be very pleasant, if it would not delay us too much."

"I have been going too fast for you. You must forgive me," Major Meredith said in a low voice, "but I do not have to tell you that every mile we put between us and Shuba increases our chance of survival."

"I realise that," she answered.

They did not speak again as that also would have been dangerous, but they sat down and after what seemed to Orissa a very short time, they moved on.

It was cold and now she could feel the wind that had come from the snows on her cheeks.

The blanket was warm as Major Meredith had anticipated, and the mere exertion of walking kept her from feeling any other discomfort than weariness.

On and on they went, climbing, descending, climbing again, keeping as much as possible high above the valley.

What was most exhausting was clambering down the sides of a gorge, which fortunately was not at this time of the year a torrent of water, and then scrambling up the other side.

They were however able to drink the clear, pure water, cold from the snows, and Major Meredith filled the water bottle.

Then at last when Orissa was beginning to feel that she would have to ask for a respite however humiliating it might be, there was a light in the East and the dawn came with incredible swiftness.

They were high on a mountain where there were great boulders, and between two of them Major Meredith found a low cave and crawled into it.

"It is quite clean," he said in a low voice and Orissa followed him on her knees.

Having passed through the entrance the cave sloped upwards. It smelt faintly of animal but it was not an unpleasant smell and on the floor there was sand that seemed to Orissa at that moment as comfortable as a feather-bed.

She sank down and without even speaking fell asleep.

She must have slept for four or five hours before she opened her eyes. At first she thought she was alone and then she realised that Major Meredith was blocking the entrance to the cave, lying flat on the ground and peering out into the sunshine.

"Can you see anything?" she asked.

He moved backwards and sat down on the floor to smile at her.

"So you are awake!" he said. "I began to think that you were Mrs. Rip Van Winkle and would sleep for a thousand years!"

"I was so tired," Orissa answered.

"You walked like a Trojan, you do not need me to tell you that!"

"Where are we?" Orissa enquired.

"That is just what I am trying to find out," he said. "I am sure you do not wish to walk one yard further than is necessary. I am going to creep out in a little while and take our bearings."

They ate some of the chapattis which had grown rather dry by now and seemed to stick in Orissa's throat. There was also a small amount of rice to go with them and this she knew was sustaining.

It would be stupid not to eat because that would only make her weaker and undoubtedly incur, if not Major Meredith's anger, his contempt.

They drank from the water-bottle which was not very large, and Major Meredith remarked that he would have to fill it again at the next stream they came to.

"What happens when you do this in the summer months?" Orissa asked.

"Then one can be very thirsty," he answered.

"I have always been told that man can survive without food, but not without water," Orissa said.

"I once resorted to milking a wild goat," Major Meredith told her. "It was an unpleasant experience which I hope not to repeat."

The brilliance of the sun was fading a little, soon the light would gather itself together in a last brilliant burst of colour before it vanished.

Major Meredith crawled through the opening of the cave.

He left his cloak behind him, but he took with him one of the sharp, strangely-shaped knives that the warlike Baluchi tribesmen always carried.

Orissa realised he must have worn it at the back of his loin-cloth.

It was so out of keeping with his impersonation of a Fakir that she was certain that he had only brought it with him as a protection because she was with him.

But she did not say anything, and when he was gone she sat thinking what a strange man he was, and how difficult she found it to understand his motives or to guess what he was thinking.

She was still smarting from his words in which he had told her plainly he had no wish to be encumbered with her, and she wondered if he really disliked her because she must hinder him in reaching his objective.

She sat thinking about him until she realised he had been gone a long time.

Had something happened to him? Suppose he had been seen by a tribesman or bitten by a snake? Could he have fallen into one of the treacherous gorges where a man who fell could so easily break his leg and lie there to die?

With what amounted to momentary panic she crept through the opening of the cave to see if she could see any sign of him.

During the heat of the afternoon she had, with his permission, taken off her turban and released her hair from the pins with which she had arranged it the night before she left the Fort.

Now she felt the faint wind stirring the darkness of her hair and turned her face towards it.

As she stood between the great boulders which were like two sentinels on either side of the cave the sun was in her eyes and as the shadow of a man's figure came round the corner she exclaimed:

"Oh, there you are! I was beginning to worry as you have been away so . . ."

The last word died on her lips as she saw the man facing her was not Major Meredith but a man with slit eyes and Mongolian features.

He was astonished at seeing her but quickly recovered himself and drew his knife from his belt lifting it high above his head.

Orissa opened her mouth to scream but no sound came. She wanted to move, to run away, but her body would not obey the commands of her brain.

She could only stand waiting for the blow. It seemed as if the man hesitated for a second, perhaps because he had not expected to find a woman in such a lonely spot.

Then even as his arm moved, Orissa saw a figure behind him and with a grunting sound the stranger fell forward to sprawl at her feet, and she saw Major Meredith's

251

knife deep in his back.

The Major drew it out, the blade now covered with blood, and struck again. Then as a crimson tide flooded over the man's clothes, Orissa put up her hands to her face to hide the horror of it.

She still could not move, but she knew that Major Meredith rose from the dead man's back and picking him up by his feet dragged him around the side of the boulder and out of her sight.

It was then, when she realised she was alone and the only evidence of what had happened was the knife lying on the ground in front of her, she crawled like a frightened animal back into the cave to sit cowering at the far end of it, her hands once again over her face.

She was shivering all over and her teeth were chattering when Major Meredith crawled into the cave and sat down beside her.

"He is dead," he said quietly. "He will not hurt you and there is no-one else about."

His voice was kind and soothing and instinctively Orissa turned towards him. He put his arm round her shoulders and held her close against him.

"It is all right," he said.

She was trembling violently, but now

because he was holding her, her teeth no longer chattered.

"I have . . . never seen anyone . . . dead before," she murmured, feeling somehow she must excuse herself.

"It is always horrifying the first time," Major Meredith said calmly, "as your father and your Uncle would tell you."

She knew he was reminding her that she belonged to the Regiment and must not behave like a coward.

"Who was . . . he? How did . . . he find . . . us?"

Major Meredith's arms seemed to tighten about her and it was curiously comforting.

"It was in actual fact the best thing that could have happened," he said.

Orissa was so surprised that she stopped trembling.

"But why?" she managed to ask.

"Because he was carrying messages to a Russian spy-ring in Peshawar."

Orissa raised her head a little.

"How do you know this?"

"He was a Tijik. Of Persian origin, they are shrewd and avaricious men who live around Kabul and do almost anything for money."

"And the Russians paid him?"

"I imagine quite a large sum by his reckoning," Major Meredith replied, "and he must have been a man they could trust because what he carried was of considerable importance."

He paused and added:

"That makes another reason why we must hurry to Peshawar as quickly as possible, and also why it is imperative that we should get there."

The calm, matter-of-fact way in which he had been speaking had swept away Orissa's panic better than if he had tried to reassure her.

Now she moved from the circle of his arms and started to pin her hair up again on top of her head, conscious that while her heart was still beating quickly she was no longer trembling.

As she did so, Major Meredith stowed away in his cloak, a number of papers she knew he had taken from the Tijik.

Then he re-tied Orissa's turban adjusting it comfortably over her hair.

"It is not too tight?" he asked.

"No."

She had the strange feeling that they might be husband and wife talking in an ordinary, unembarrassed way as he helped her dress.

There was no time for further conversation as the light had now gone and they were once again on their way.

They walked and walked! The route, Orissa thought, was far harder than it had been the night before, but perhaps it seemed so because she was already tired.

Despite her slippers, the stones seemed to cut into the soles of her feet, and she had long ago worn away the wool covering that Major Meredith had placed over them, so that loose strands of it flapped around her bare ankles.

The night before had been chill, but there had been very little wind. Tonight, unexpectedly, a gale blew up soon after midnight.

It was gusty, violent and seemed to whistle around the mountain peaks to cut icily into their bones.

It blew Major Meredith's cloak out behind him like the sails of a ship, and Orissa wondered how he could bear the cold of it on his naked body.

She herself felt as if her woollen cloak were made of paper and soon her hands were frozen so that it was difficult to move her fingers.

Tonight Major Meredith suggested no respite but strode ahead until Orissa found herself half running because she was so afraid he would disappear into the darkness and she would be left alone.

They climbed up — they climbed down. They rounded great boulders. They even on one occasion walked along the knife-edge of a precipice which fell for hundreds of feet below them, and Orissa felt at any moment she might go hurtling down into the depths below.

She longed to tell Major Meredith she could not face it. It was too much to ask of anyone, let alone a woman! Then a pride greater than she knew she possessed made her force herself not to speak of her fears.

"Face the rock — hold on to it! Move your feet sideways, one by one," he commanded her.

She obeyed him, and hated him because she felt he was ordering her about as if she were a sepoy under his command and she had no will of her own.

Only once when she collected a stone in her shoe and had to shake it out did she cry after him to wait.

"What is it? What is the matter?" he asked and she heard the irritation in his voice.

"It is a stone," she answered, sitting down to take off her shoe, shake it and put it back on her foot which was so cold she hardly knew she had a covering for it.

"We cannot wait," he admonished.

"No, of course not," she answered obediently.

They climbed up what seemed to Orissa the barren side of a cliff without a foot-hold and then up another to walk on and on, until finally she knew that the cold had frozen not only her body but her brain.

She could no longer think, no longer force herself to follow the flapping cloak ahead of her.

'Let him go without me,' she told herself. 'It is no use. I cannot do it, I cannot!'

She had not spoken, but perhaps some sixth sense told him what she was feeling, because Major Meredith turned round suddenly.

By the light of the stars he could see her small, sagging figure, her eyes dark with pain.

He did not speak. He merely picked her up in his arms.

Orissa wanted to protest. She wanted to tell him she could manage on her own, but the words would not come. She was too cold — too utterly and completely exhausted.

She put her face against his shoulder and thought if she died at this moment it did not matter . . .

■ ■ ■ ■

Orissa was conscious of feeling warm.

Her cheeks were no longer frozen in a face that was made of ice. Her hands were warm and her whole body was relaxed.

Somewhere a clock seemed to be ticking . . . she wondered vaguely what it could be.

It was so wonderful to be warm again and it seemed as if she had been happy in her dreams and the feeling of happiness was still with her.

Then suddenly she realised that her cheek was against Major Meredith's chest and it was the warmth of his bare skin she felt.

One hand was on his naked body and the other was also pressed against him tucked between her breasts.

It was very dark and she realised that he had covered her with his cloak which enveloped her like a tent in a warm, almost stifling, darkness, and the sound she could hear was his heart beating.

It was not only an incredible relief to be warm, but also a feeling of joy she could not express to know that he held her close against him so that she was safe and protected.

Then in that moment she knew she loved him!

She knew it as if a star had fallen out of the sky and told her so or a meteor had shot across the firmament.

She loved him! For the moment nothing else mattered!

She shut her eyes and went to sleep again . . .

It must have been hours later that she felt him stir and when he drew the cloak from off her head she felt the air was hot and knew that the sun was up.

Because she felt shy at the manner in which she had slept, she pretended still to be asleep.

Very gently he moved his arm from under her and laid her down on the floor. Then so quietly she could hardly hear him, she knew that he went from the cave, or wherever it was they had slept, and she was alone.

Very cautiously she opened her eyes.

It was another cave as she had expected. Quite a big one. Much bigger than the one they had been in the previous night.

Orissa gave a little sigh.

Everything came flooding back into her memory. The terrible cold and the moment that she had collapsed and Major Meredith had been aware of it; her waking to know that she was held closely against him and that she loved him.

'How can I love him?' she asked herself. 'All I am to him is an irritation!'

Once he had kissed her and she knew now as she had really known at the time that for him it had not been a moment of importance, but merely of amusement.

She was well aware how terrible she must look now with her skin dyed brown, her hair hidden under a faded, ragged turban, her legs encased in what remained of the rough, coarse wool.

She remembered that if they reached safety and her Uncle and his beleaguered force were relieved, he had promised her the most beautiful gowns that he could buy in Lahore, Delhi and Madras.

When she wore them, would Major Meredith find her attractive? She rather doubted it. She had a feeling that she was not the type of woman that he admired.

Adventurous men did not want adventurous wives. They wanted quiet, clinging little women who sat at home and waited placidly for them to return.

It all seemed hopeless, Orissa thought. Then as Major Meredith came back into the cave she felt her heart leap and turn over in her breast.

He might look strange and peculiar; he might be harsh and ruthless; he might have killed a man in front of her; and yet she loved him!

She loved him in a manner which she knew instinctively was not just the romantic emotion of a young girl who knew nothing about men, but the love of a woman for a man to whom she had given not only her heart but her soul.

'I love you! . . . I love you!' she wanted to say to him.

Instead she managed to ask quite unemotionally:

"How far did we manage to go last night?"

"Quite a considerable distance," Major Meredith replied. "We are now back on the mountains that border the Peshawar road. Far enough away, I think, to be safe from the tribesmen encircling the Fort."

Orissa looked at him with gladness in her eyes and then she said a little hesitatingly:

"I am . . . sorry you had to . . . carry me last night. It was . . . so cold."

As she spoke she felt the blood rise in her cheeks because of the method by which he had warmed her. But she told herself that the dye on her face would hide her blushes from him.

"I pushed you too hard," he said. "It was

cruel, but there was nothing else I could do."

"No, I understand that," Orissa agreed.

"Do I have to tell you that you have been absolutely wonderful?" he asked.

There was a note in his voice which made her glance at him quickly and then look away.

". . . failed you," she said almost in a whisper.

"You did nothing of the sort!" he retorted. "No other woman in the world could have done better."

It was impossible to look at him, almost impossible to breathe. Then he said in a different tone altogether:

"I apologise. I should have given you something to eat. We are getting rather short, but with any luck it should last us so that we do not actually starve before we reach Peshawar."

Orissa thought that the chapattis, and even the rice, by this time were inedible. But she forced mouthful after mouthful down her throat with the help of sips of water and tried not to acknowledge that she was very hungry.

Their meal finished, Major Meredith went to the mouth of the cave.

"There is a shepherd down below with a

flock of sheep. I am going to take a risk and start walking again now before nightfall."

"Is that wise?" she asked.

"It is imperative we get to Peshawar as soon as possible," he answered. "The messenger I bribed may not have got through and God knows what is happening at Shuba."

Orissa knew that this thought had been haunting him and she felt as if she had not been as deeply perturbed as she should have been about her Uncle.

As if to make up for her omission she prayed passionately that the assault on the Fort had not begun and that somehow, although she had no idea how, they would be able to get reinforcements through.

"Yes, let us go at once," she said and without saying any more they set out.

The strongest heat of the day was past, but it was still very hot and soon Orissa found the woollen cloak she was carrying intolerably heavy on her arm.

At the same time she dared not throw it away. She knew that it would be cold again at night and without it she might easily get pneumonia.

To be ill would be even worse than being exhausted.

Now instead of suffering from extreme

cold, Orissa could feel the sweat running down her back and between her breasts.

She longed to take off her turban, but she knew that Major Meredith would be angry if she even suggested such an idea.

They must still keep up their disguise.

The back of her legs were aching intolerably and she knew that the shoes that she wore were in tatters.

They climbed and descended, slithered down steep gorges, had a drink from the rapidly dwindling streams, struggled up the other side, until as they rounded what seemed to Orissa almost the peak of a high mountain, she saw Major Meredith in front of her stop dead.

As she came up to him, she too stood paralysed at what she saw.

Coming along the tiny goats' path on which they were walking and covering the side of the hill there were men — hundreds of men — looking for the moment like ants as they advanced at an almost incredible speed.

"What is . . . it? Who are . . . they?" Orissa tried to say.

Then as she expected Major Meredith to turn round, to run, to make some attempt to hide from the oncoming horde, she realised incredulously that the men approaching were wearing uniforms.

They were all dressed alike and on the side of their dark heads was a cap she recognised.

She heard Major Meredith give a shout of sheer joy and fling up his arms! Even as he did so, Orissa knew that not only were they saved but so was Shuba.

They were the Ghurkas!

The tough, hard-fighting, mountain-climbing little soldiers of Nepal were on their way to the rescue!

CHAPTER NINE

Orissa walked across the garden and the sun was warm on her bare head.

There was a place hidden away behind the rhododendron bushes where there was a little Indian God set on a stone pillar against the green of the shrubs.

The figure was very old and must have been stolen at some time from a Temple.

She knew it represented Krishna, the God of Love and as she sat looking at it, she found herself praying that He would bring her the love she needed so desperately.

It was hard even now to realise that once they had reached Peshawar Major Meredith had disappeared and she had not seen him or heard of him since.

After they had talked with the Ghurkas on the mountainside, and Major Meredith had explained to their Commander the exact position of the tribesmen encamped around the Fort, they had slithered straight down the other side of the hill onto the Peshawar road.

There they found the brakes and wagons which had carried the Ghurkas from the British Cantonment at Peshawar.

Orissa learnt that another Battalion had ascended the mountains on the other side of the road so that they could converge simultaneously on the tribesmen.

"As soon as the road is clear," Major Meredith told her, "it has been arranged for a Battalion of 43rd Light Foot to re-inforce the troops in the Fort."

"Who thought of sending the Ghurkas?" Orissa asked.

Major Meredith smiled.

"I knew that two Battalions of their Regiment were at Peshawar."

She had however little chance of any private conversation with him.

They had been driven to the British Cantonment in an Army brake drawn by four horses, and while it was not very comfortable it was certainly quicker than and much preferable to walking.

Fortunately they arrived late, long after it was dark, as Orissa was well aware how peculiar she must look dressed in a Ghurka Officer's greatcoat.

But it did in fact cover her legs. Major

Meredith, having removed his wig, was forced to resort to all sorts of strange clothing to keep himself warm.

It had been exhilarating to drive beside him on the high-box seat of the Army brake, but they were sitting next to the Ghurka driver and there were two soldiers behind them, so it was impossible to say very much to each other.

Major Meredith had given Orissa into the charge of an Officer's wife.

"Feed her and let her sleep!" he said.

Orissa thought afterwards that it sounded rather as if he were giving instructions about a dog or a horse!

However it was not difficult to obey him, for now that the excitement was over Orissa felt more exhausted than ever before in her whole life.

She could hardly keep her eyes open to eat the food that was provided, and when eventually she crawled into bed it was to fall immediately into a deep, dreamless sleep.

She slept well into the next day, and when she finally awoke it was to find Major Meredith had disappeared.

No-one volunteered any information as to whether he had gone back to Shuba or perhaps to some high-up Army Commander with the papers he had taken from the man he had killed.

Orissa was too shy to ask questions, yet she longed with an ever-increasing ache in her heart for news of him.

She was not permitted to stay in the British Cantonment at Peshawar but was sent South to Lahore.

It was a delight to be again in the town where she had lived as a child.

It was still as she remembered it with avenues of trees, luxurious foliage and roses growing in an incredible profusion.

But not even the joy of meeting some of the people who remembered her mother, and of visiting places that had remained vividly in her memory all through the years, could assuage the restlessness she felt.

It was difficult for her to settle to anything.

She did learn however, that the Ghurkas had arrived at Shuba in time. Faced with fighters even more war-like and aggressive than themselves, the tribesmen had fled back into the hills from which they had come.

Shuba had been reinforced. Her Uncle was in good health.

She had a letter from him saying how proud he was of her and how much he was looking forward to seeing her again.

She had expected to wait for him in Lahore because that was where the Royal Chilterns were usually stationed and the Colonel's house was all ready for him to return to it.

But just as Orissa was wondering how she could contrive to leave her kindly Hostess, who was the wife of the Second-in-Command, and move into the house where she anticipated she would in the future, play hostess for her Uncle, she received an invitation.

It was from the Colonel of the Bengal Lancers, saying that he and his wife were going on holiday to their house in the foothills of the Himalayas and inviting her to stay with them.

The mere name of the Regiment made Orissa's hopes rise that it was Major Meredith who had arranged this and that she would find him waiting for her when she reached the Colonel's residence.

She was however disappointed.

The house was set amid the most exquisite scenery just above a large lake, with the hills rising high behind it.

It was the sort of place in which all those who were stationed in India liked their wives and families to stay during the heat of the summer, and dreamed about when even the punkas could not stir the torrid air.

But to Orissa it seemed only an empty shell because here again there was no sign of Major Meredith.

She had also a very disquieting conversation with her hostess, Mrs. Lawrence.

"I am sure Myron Meredith will be decorated for the splendid way in which he saved Shuba," she remarked conversationally to Orissa.

"Decorated?" Orissa questioned.

"He has deserved one for a long time but as I expect you know, my dear, those who take part in the 'Great Game' are seldom rewarded for their work."

Orissa did not reply and Mrs. Lawrence went on to say:

"My husband is so fond of Myron and it would be a tragedy if he had to leave India."

"Why should he do . . . that?" Orissa asked feeling it was hard to say the words.

"I believe that his father, — Lord Croome, is very ill," Mrs. Lawrence answered, "and when Myron comes into the title it is doubtful if he will wish to stay on in the Regiment. I imagine he will have too much to occupy him at home."

Orissa felt as if the information was like an icy hand laid upon her heart.

Suppose, she asked herself, that night as

she lay awake staring into the darkness, Major Meredith went back to England and she never saw him again.

With all the questions with which she had tortured herself, she had not anticipated anything like this. She felt despairingly that their ways had now separated and Fate was no longer bringing them together.

She had thought secretly in her heart that she could not escape him, but now it appeared as if there was a great gulf dividing them.

Once again she asked herself desperately why she should mean anything to him. First he had despised her, then she had been an encumbrance, someone to whom he had done his duty faultlessly, but was no longer of any importance to him.

Walking across the garden now she did not see its beauty.

The beds were full of English flowers cultivated by Mrs. Lawrence to remind her of home. There were pansies and marigolds, sweet-smelling pinks, wall-flowers, and forget-me-nots all growing in an over-luxuriant profusion.

Each one of them was a tiny piece of England for those in whom they aroused an irrepressible nostalgia.

The little stone image of Krishna danced

joyously on his pillar but Orissa felt almost as if he mocked her, telling her of a happiness and love which she would never know.

It was very quiet in the hidden place she had made her own and to which she came for comfort.

There was only the song of the birds and the buzz of the bees, and hovering over the blossoms of the shrubs a crowd of brilliantly coloured butterflies.

Somewhere far away a man was singing a love song. Orissa knew the music although she could not quite hear the words. Perhaps it was a plea to Krishna as so many love songs were!

"There is a letter for you, Lady Orissa," someone said.

Orissa looked round to see that Captain Radhi, one of Colonel Lawrence's native officers, had approached without her hearing him.

"It is from your Uncle, Colonel Hobart," he smiled. "It came with some despatches."

"Thank you" Orissa answered.

Then because she could not help the words bursting from her lips she asked:

"Is there any news of . . . Major Meredith?"

The Indian officer seemed to hesitate.

He was a handsome young man with dark,

eloquent eyes which were always full of admiration for Orissa.

"There is a rumour from Peshawar," he said slowly, "that he has been — killed!"

Orissa was very still.

For a moment she could feel nothing, not even pain. It was as if the whole world was silent.

"But I am sure it is only a rumour," Captain Radhi continued quickly, "and the Major will turn up when we least expect it. He always does!"

He walked away without saying any more.

Orissa put her letter unopened down on the seat beside her, and then as she stared at the little Krishna, tears filled her eyes.

This was the end!

This was what she had always been afraid might happen! This was why she had lain awake night after night, staring into the darkness. She knew that without him she had no wish to go on living.

Now the singer must have come nearer and she could hear the words of the love song. Orissa translated them to herself.

And after death in the Great To-Be
Where dwell the Gods who make our
    Laws,
I, when you come to seek for me,

Am, ever and always, only yours.

The words seemed to express the agony in her heart.

"Oh, Lord Krishna," she prayed, "let me find him again . . . let me find him . . . and one day . . . give me his . . . heart . . . as he has mine!"

She thought for one moment that the stone face of the dancing God turned — beautiful, golden, shining, liquid eyed, He smiled at her.

Then her eyes were blinded by her tears and her cheeks were wet with them.

Suddenly a deep voice behind her exclaimed:

"Crying? I have never known you cry, Orissa!"

She started to her feet thinking she must be dreaming and saw him standing against the rhododendrons.

He was in uniform, but bare headed, and his grey eyes looked into hers just as they had done every night in her dreams.

"You are alive! You are alive!"

She ran towards him as she spoke and without conscious thought, merely because it was where she longed to be, she was in his arms.

He held her very tightly and, as she

thought it was like reaching Heaven itself, his lips were on hers.

He kissed her as he had done the night on board ship, but now it was more wonderful, more spiritual, more vivid than anything she had imagined or remembered.

Something like quick-silver swept through her body as she felt he took not only her heart but her soul from between her lips and made it his.

Then he was kissing the tears from her cheeks, her wet eyes and again her mouth, until the whole world ceased to exist and there was nothing left but him.

When at length Orissa could speak her face was radiant and her eyes were shining as if they were filled with sunshine.

"They told . . . me you were . . . dead!"

"Forgive me, my darling, I did not mean to upset you so much."

Orissa stiffened in his arms.

"You . . . told the Captain to tell me . . . that?"

"Yes."

"But how . . . could you when it was a . . . lie?"

"You must forgive me."

"But why? Why? Why did you want to . . . trick me in such a . . . cruel manner?"

"It was wrong of me," he admitted, "but I

wanted to bring to the surface what I knew existed between us. I wanted to be sure that you loved me enough."

He paused.

"Enough for what?" Orissa asked.

"For us to be married at once! Now!"

Orissa looked at him, her eyes very wide and wondering in her small face.

"I have to go home, my darling. My father is dead!"

"I am . . . sorry," Orissa murmured.

"He wanted to die — he was in great pain. He knew that he would not live long but he hated what he called 'mourning and misery'."

He paused to continue:

"That is why he sent me back to India, and I travelled on the same ship as you."

"So you are . . . leaving . . . India?"

It was hard to say the words even though she was close against him, and waves of happiness seemed to sweep over her as if they came from a flood-tide that was irresistible.

"Only for a short while," he answered, "but I cannot leave you behind."

"Do you . . . really want . . . me?"

"More than I have ever wanted anything in my whole life before! So I have made plans, my precious, to which I hope you will agree."

"I will agree to . . . anything," Orissa cried passionately, "as long as I can be with . . . you."

"That is what I wanted you to say," he answered, "but there was no time to court you as I should have done."

He gave her a little smile with the twist to his lips which she remembered so well.

"I apologise for needling you emotionally but it was essential if we were to be married at once and have just a week's honeymoon before we travel home."

He sensed there was a faint cloud in Orissa's eyes at the thought of returning to England, and he said softly:

"Shall I make you happy, my Sweetheart, by telling you it will not be for long? I am to be offered a new position in India, one where I think it would be extremely advantageous to have a wife who not only loves the country but also speaks Urdu."

"A new position?" Orissa queried. "What is it?"

"The Viceroy has told me that Her Majesty wishes to appoint me as Lieutenant-Governor of the North-West Provinces!"

He felt Orissa draw in her breath and he added:

"Will that please you, my adventurous little love?"

"You know," Orissa said and now once again there were tears in her eyes, "that I could not think of anything more perfect, more absolutely wonderful, than to be with . . . you and for . . . us to be in India."

Orissa stood on the verandah and looked into the garden.

She could not have believed that anything could be so beautiful.

Rhododendrons — crimson, pink, red, vermilion and white, swept up the hillside behind the small bungalow towards the great sun-capped mountains which lay behind them.

In the garden itself there was a profusion of flowers of every sort and colour from the scented orchid to the sweet fragrance of the lily-of-the-valley.

The birds were singing their evening hymn of praise, and Orissa had a glimpse of a Himalayan pheasant scuttling through the blossom-laden shrubs, the bird with the most brilliant plumage in the world.

From the servants' quarters at the back of the bungalow which Myron had been lent for their honeymoon, she could hear the soft chatter of sing-song voices and the creak of the water-wheel as the fat, old buffalo plodded round and round to bring the water to the surface.

It was all so lovely, so dear and so familiar that she held her breath in case it should prove to be a mirage that would vanish suddenly before her eyes.

She was wearing a turquoise-blue sari deeply embroidered with silver thread and pearls and around her neck there was a turquoise and diamond necklace.

They had both been part of her wedding gifts from her husband and on her finger also set with diamonds was an enormous turquoise, the stone which all over the East is considered lucky.

She had been married in a simple white muslin gown in the nearest Church to the Lawrences' house. The only witnesses had been the Colonel and his wife.

Afterwards they had driven away, but the last part of their journey had been on the backs of sure-footed little mountain ponies.

Every moment their surroundings had grown more beautiful. Every twist and turn of the mountain path had made Orissa think she was drawing nearer to Paradise.

'I am married . . . I have found love . . . we are together!' she had whispered to herself, vividly conscious of the man riding with her.

Now she heard his footsteps behind her

on the verandah and she felt as if every nerve in her body tingled with her awareness of him.

He came to her side.

"It is so beautiful, so incredibly, unbelievably beautiful!" she said softly.

"That is what I thought, when I first saw you."

She turned her head to look up at him and felt she could not breathe because of the expression in his eyes.

"You despised me!" she said. "I saw the . . . contempt in your face!"

"I still thought you beautiful," he answered, "which was why it hurt me that you were involved in anything so unsavoury as an intrigue."

"And yet you . . . kissed me that night on the . . . ship."

"I could not help myself," he said, "you were so exquisitely lovely as you turned your face up to the stars. Then, as you are well aware, Orissa, something happened we could neither of us forget."

"I did not know a . . . kiss could be like . . . that."

"Nor did I, and afterwards when I knew that spiritually we belonged to each other, you drove me mad with jealousy. If you only knew how the thought of that husband in the East India Company tortured me."

Orissa gave a little laugh and slipped her hand into his.

"And . . . now?" she asked her eyes on his face.

He was about to reply when the bearer behind them said:

"Dinner is served, Mem-Sahib."

Hand-in-hand they went into the Dining-Room.

They were waited on by two servants and ate the dishes which Orissa loved: trout from the streams running down from the snows, hot curries with the little bowls of colourful spices, fruits that had been picked that very morning from the tree.

It was dark when dinner was finished and they talked together for a long time.

The candles on the table glinted on Orissa's necklace and brought out the lights in her hair in which, Indian fashion, she had arranged a spray of fragrant tuberoses.

It was so wonderful to know that their minds were in accord, that they stimulated each other's thoughts, and that there were a million subjects to explore together.

But there were also little pregnant silences when Orissa knew that heart spoke to heart and there was no need for words.

At last Myron pushed back his chair and

putting his arm around Orissa's shoulders drew her out onto the verandah again.

It was not cold. The heat of the day had passed to leave behind the gentle coolness of a summer's night in England.

It was very quiet. The birds had gone to rest and stars bestrewed the sky, glittering like jewels against a velvet background. There was a crescent moon high over the furthest mountain peak.

"Do you still feel small, insignificant and lonely?" he asked.

"Not any more," Orissa replied, "not when I am . . . close to you, when I know that at last I . . . belong."

"We have always belonged to each other," he answered. "This is not the first time we have met, Orissa, nor will it be the last. You are indivisibly a part of me as I am a part of you."

"Mr. Mahla was right," Orissa said softly. "He said that our Fate . . . our Karma . . . was written and we could do nothing about it."

"I have no wish to alter mine," Myron said softly.

As he spoke he put his fingers under Orissa's chin and turned her face up to his.

For a moment he looked down into the darkness of her eyes and then his mouth was on hers and he held her captive.

She knew then there was no escape even if she had wished it.

They were an absolute part of each other and nothing could separate them.

"I love you!" he said and she heard the passion in his voice. "God, how I love you, and how much I have wanted you since the first moment we saw each other!"

"I think I knew when you . . . kissed me that I would never be . . . complete unless I belonged to you."

"As you do now, my darling," he said. "You are mine! Mine, and nothing can ever separate us."

He kissed her until she felt that the world whirled around her, that the stars fell from the sky to encircle them, and her lips were no longer her own but his.

"I love . . . you," she whispered, "I did not believe that such . . . happiness was possible."

He could feel her quivering against him, and he knew from the new depth in her voice and the response of her lips that he had aroused a flame within her to complement the burning desire in himself.

"I will look after you, protect you, and worship you, not only in this life, but in all our lives to come," he vowed.

"It is . . . Karma," she whispered.

"The Karma of Love!"

As he spoke he drew her close against his heart and through the open window into the darkness of the bedroom.

The white mosquito netting was draped high on the canopy above the bed. It was not necessary at this time of year, but it looked like the gossamer sails of a fairy ship.

Myron stopped in the centre of the room and very gently he unclasped the turquoise necklace he had given Orissa.

Then he took the tuberoses from her hair and the pins which held it in place. The long dark strands fell over her shoulders almost to her waist.

He kissed one.

"When I held you in my arms in the cave," he said, "your hair smelt of jasmine. It has haunted me ever since."

She could not speak, and she felt his hands draw away the turquoise sari which fell in a silken pool at her feet.

The moonlight coming through the window enveloped her with its silver light, and she stood like a lotus bloom coming into flower.

She was not shy, the magic of Krishna had caught her up into an ecstasy of wonder, so that she was one with the mountains, the snowy peaks, the star-strewn sky, the gods.

Myron stood looking at her and held his breath.

"Could anyone be so beautiful?" he asked hoarsely. "Are you real or only a dream?"

As if her voice came from a long distance, she whispered:

"I am . . . ever and always . . . only yours."

Then his mouth took possession of her and his heart was on hers.

ABOUT THE AUTHOR

Barbara Cartland who sadly died in May 2000 at the age of nearly 99 was the world's most famous romantic novelist who wrote 723 books in her lifetime with worldwide sales of over 1 billion copies and her books were translated into 36 different languages.

As well as romantic novels, she wrote historical biographies, 6 autobiographies, theatrical plays, books of advice on life, love, vitamins and cookery. She also found time to be a political speaker and television and radio personality.

She wrote her first book at the age of 21 and this was called *Jigsaw.* It became an immediate bestseller and sold 100,000 copies in hardback and was translated into 6 different languages. She wrote continuously throughout her life, writing bestsellers for an astonishing 76 years. Her books have always been immensely popular in the United States, where in 1976 her current books were at numbers 1 & 2 in the B. Dalton bestsellers list, a feat never achieved before or since by any author.

Barbara Cartland became a legend in her own lifetime and will be best remembered for her wonderful romantic novels, so loved by her millions of readers throughout the world.

Her books will always be treasured for their moral message, her pure and innocent heroines, her good looking and dashing heroes and above all her belief that the power of love is more important than anything else in everyone's life.

We hope you have enjoyed this Large Print book. Other Thorndike, Wheeler, and Chivers Press Large Print books are available at your library or directly from the publishers.

For information about current and upcoming titles, please call or write, without obligation, to:

Publisher
Thorndike Press
295 Kennedy Memorial Drive
Waterville, ME 04901
Tel. (800) 223-1244

or visit our Web site at:

www.gale.com/thorndike
www.gale.com/wheeler

OR

Chivers Large Print
published by BBC Audiobooks Ltd
St James House, The Square
Lower Bristol Road
Bath BA2 3SB
England
Tel. +44(0) 800 136919
email: bbcaudiobooks@bbc.co.uk
www.bbcaudiobooks.co.uk

All our Large Print titles are designed for easy reading, and all our books are made to last.